Detour

Black Curtain Press
PO Box 632
Floyd VA 24091

ISBN 10:1-61720-932-5
ISBN 13: 978-1-61720-932-1

First Edition
10 9 8 7 6 5 4 3 2 1

Detour

Martin M. Goldsmith

I. ALEXANDER ROTH

The big grey roadster streaked by me and came to a halt fifty yards down the highway with screaming tires. I got my lungs full of the smell of hot oil and burning rubber. It choked me so that for a full minute I couldn't breathe. Neither could I move; I just stood there staring stupidly at it and at the two black skid-marks the wheels left on the concrete. I was heading west, via the thumb-route, and had been waiting over three hours for a lift. I can't remember exactly where I was at the time, but it was somewhere in New Mexico, between Las Cruces and Lordsburg.

It seemed sort of crazy, that car stopping. I had begun to believe that only old jalopies and trucks picked up hikers any more. Bums are generally pretty dirty and good cars have nice seats. Then, too, it was a lonesome stretch in there and plenty can happen on a lonesome stretch.

The guy driving the car yelled at me over his shoulder. "Hey, you! Are you coming?" He acted as though he was in a great hurry, for he goosed his engine impatiently so I'd shake a leg.

I snapped out of it. It was hot as a bastard and I guess the sun was getting me. Somewhere back along the line I had lost my hat and the top of my head seemed to be on fire. Anyway, the last two hours I had been waving cars more or less mechanically, not expecting anyone to stop. A few hundred of them must have whizzed by without even slowing down a little to give me the once-over. You know, hitch-hiking isn't as popular out west as it used to be. I suppose that is why the real bums stick to the rails.

"I'm coming, I'm coming!" I shouted as loud as I could. My throat was caked with road dust and even opening my mouth was painful. It felt like someone had given my tonsils a good going over with sandpaper. Taking the lead out of my pants, I broke all records running to the car and piling in, lugging my valise after me. "Sorry, mister. The heat's got me down."

The man reached back, pressed a button behind his seat and the rumble popped open. He pointed to my valise. I tossed it in and slammed the rumble shut.

"Make sure your door's closed, Johnny." I made sure.

We drove along for a little while, neither one of us saying anything. I was glad of that. I never know what to say to strange people driving cars, except the old line of gab which is flat as hell. The chances are a guy knows just as well as you do that it is a nice day, that the scenery is pretty, that the road is quite rough in spots and that it can't be much farther to Deming. Then, too, you never can tell if a fellow wants to talk. A lot of rides have been cut short because of a big mouth.

I was sweating like a man in a Turkish bath, so I kept to my own side of the car. My dirty polo-shirt clung to my back as though it was glued there and I could feel little drops of perspiration trickle down my legs into what was left of my socks. On either side of the road baked endless low hills covered with green sage. Every thing in sight reflected a glare in spite of the thick coating of dust which had settled even on the highway itself. The top was down on the car, but to catch some breeze I had to hold my head out over the wind-wing. We were making better than seventy miles an hour with the road full of curves, yet I was too grateful for the air to be nervous. As I cooled off a bit I took back all the names I had been calling the Southwest.

"How far are you going?" he asked me after a while.

"L.A."

The man turned to face me in surprise. "Well, you're really traveling, aren't you?"

"Yeah," I answered him, "but I don't expect to make it for a couple of years at the rate I've been promoting rides."

"Not much luck?"

I thought I'd make him feel good. They tell me that is the secret of success—you know, winning friends and influencing people. From the looks of the buggy, I figured this guy should be good for a hamburger.

"There ain't many people driving cars," I said, "who will stop and pick up a fellow these days."

He ran a sleeve across his sun-glasses to wipe off the dust.

"No, I guess not."

"They're afraid of a stick-up, maybe. It's only men who have been around that can tell a straight from a phony." I thought that ought to hold him for a while.

"Where are you coming from?"

"Detroit. "

I don't know why I said that; there really was no call to lie. Maybe I was so accustomed to lying it had become a habit, I don't know. But that's me all over. For the life of me, I can't figure myself out. The fact of the matter was I hadn't been anywhere near Detroit for years.

"Detroit, eh?"

"Yes, sir." I said it, so I had to stick to it.

"Well, Detroit, you're in luck this time. I'm going all the way."

I couldn't believe my ears. I thought I was dreaming.

"You mean you're going straight through to Los Angeles?"

"That's the ticket. Can you drive a car?"

"Sure thing," I breathed, trying to keep from singing or something.

"Good."

"Whenever you're tired, let me know."

"I'll holler."

He didn't say anything after that for a couple of miles and I slumped back on the rich leather upholstery and got to thinking all the hell I'd been through and how nice it was that it was practically over. Since losing my job playing fiddle in Bellman's band, a lot of water had gone under the bridge. I didn't mind losing the job so much—because with me or without me Bellman's band was pretty punk—but Sue ought never to have walked out like that only a week or ten days before we were slated to get married. The idea of me being unemployed was nothing for her to tear her hair out because I can handle a fiddle well enough to land something in a minute, providing there is a spot open; but what got me was that she was practically postponing our marriage for years. With everything all set, she certainly picked a fine time to go to Hollywood. Well, I told myself, what the devil. She didn't mean anything by it. Sue was an impulsive kid, jumping at the first thing that came along.

That got me to thinking: maybe that was how she agreed to marry me. I had an apartment and forty a week coming in and... But no. It was a dirty thing to think, and it didn't stand up. Sue could have had Bellman if she'd wanted him. She could have had any fellow in the band.

Of course all the hell wasn't over yet by a long shot. Just reaching L.A. didn't mean I had a job and a bank account; but at least the long trip would be over and I'd be with Sue again and there'd be no more hoofing it down the concrete or parking my can on guard-railings. You can lay your bottom dollar the next time I take it into my head to go somewhere I won't blow my money—or, if I do, at least I'll stick around until I can dig up the price of a bus.

We took a curve fast. The rear-end skidded on the smooth surface of the road. I was a little scared. I don't mind fast driving when I'm at the wheel, but I didn't know this guy. A couple of feet to the right was one hell of a ravine and I kept imagining we were edging towards it. One wrong move of the hand could have sent us into eternity, Kingdom Come, or whatever is waiting for us. I glanced at the speedometer and saw the needle hovering at seventy-eight, then eighty. Boy, that was some car all right. It was a year old, but it seemed like Cinderella's coach after that Model T fertilizer truck I'd ridden all the way from El Paso. I still smelled like a barn. The man at the wheel must have noticed me watching the dash. "I started from New York," he volunteered. "Only four and a half days so far."

"Some driving," I commented. The way I said it could have meant almost anything. I'm from New York myself and I know how most of them drive. However, in a few minutes I was considerably relieved. Here was one New Yorker who really could drive. I admired the dexterous way he used his hands and feet as he double clutched into second at seventy to save his brakes at a cow-crossing. It was then that I first got a flash of the deep scratches on his right wrist. They were wicked marks—three puffy red lines, about a quarter of an inch part.

Without removing his eyes from the road, for which I was grateful, he said, "Aren't they beauties? Those are going to be scars some day. What an animal!"

I'd seen plenty of scars before in my life—from old war wounds and appendicitis incisions to the long whip-welts on an ex-con I knew who'd once been on a Florida chain-gang—but these scratches interested me. "What kind of an animal was it, sir?" I asked. "Must have been pretty big and vicious to have done that."

He laughed. "Right on both counts, Detroit. I was wrestling with the most dangerous animal in the world. A woman." He laughed again. This time I joined him. "She must have been Tarzan's mate," I said. "It looks like you lost the bout."

"Oh, I'm always getting cut and scratched, seems to me. I can't even shave myself without losing a quart of blood. Have to go to a barber. But if you want to see a real scar, take a look at this." He pulled the right sleeve of his coat up a little higher and I almost got sick to my stomach. The thing looked like a thick piece of twine twisted around his forearm. It was rough and had a lot of little bumps and knots on it. "I got that one dueling," he explained.

"Dueling!"

Say, what kind of a chump did this fellow take me for, anyway? Only Germans dueled any more, and I could tell just by looking at him he wasn't German.

"Yes," he went on. "Of course we were only kids. My dad owned a couple of Franco-Prussian sabers. Kept them on the wall for a decoration. Well, another kid and I took them out one day when he wasn't around and had a duel. He got me on the arm here. It was a mean cut. An infection set in later."

"Yeah." I can see."

"Some beauty-mark, eh?"

I turned my head away and the man pulled down his sleeve. Then he lapsed into silence, his mouth drawn into a thin, tight line. I wondered what he was thinking about, or if I had said something wrong. Some guys are sensitive. Maybe I should have told him the scar was gorgeous?

But in a minute he continued, "The pain made me crazy and I lost my head, I guess. I began slashing, and before I knew it I... I put the other kid's eye out."

He whipped the Buick around a sharp bend with a yank at the wheel. The rear tires screeched to beat the band. We must have lost at least a half-inch of rubber on that turn and I was beginning to think that maybe I'd never see Sue in Los Angeles at that.

"Gee," I said solemnly, "that was tough."

"Oh, it was an accident, of course. But you know how kids are. I got frightened and decided to run away from home. My father almost caught me while I was packing my duds. If the bloody rag I wrapped around my wrist hadn't attracted his attention he would sure as hell have seen my bundle. I sneaked away while he was calling the doctor."

He paused to light himself a cigarette which he took from a case in the dash-compartment. I was hoping he'd offer me one, but he didn't.

"That was fifteen years ago," he said. "I haven't been home since."

I couldn't think of anything to say to that at the moment; I had my mind on bumming one of his butts. If he had only been going a few miles I would have risked making a pest of myself; but this guy was my one chance of getting to Hollywood before next Christmas. I made up my mind to forget about a smoke.

"Well, what do you know about that," I murmured, trying to appear interested as hell. "Can you beat it?" He was smoking expensive Egyptians.

About two hours later we hit Lordsburg and the owner of the car pulled up before a restaurant on the main drag. Although it was late afternoon, the sun was still shining as bright and as hot as ever; and when the stranger removed his sunglasses he had two round white patches circling his eyes. He mopped his burned face with a handkerchief. I wanted to mop mine, too; but my one and only handkerchief was split in half and being used to plug up the holes in my shoes.

"Hungry, Detroit?"

Was I hungry? Well I certainly should have been. I hadn't had anything to eat since the midnight doughnut and coffee I'd managed to chisel seventeen hours before. I was almost at the point of wishing I was back in the can at Dallas, where at least a fellow could have something to eat twice a day. Yet, even with that rotten gnawing in the pit of my stomach, I didn't want to be in too big a rush to put on the feedbag. First I had to make sure that this fellow knew the score. If I got him down on me it was good-bye ticket to Hollywood.

"I'll wait for you out here in the car, mister," I

mumbled, trying to look as forlorn as possible—without hamming it. It was a big moment. Believe me, if the stranger had shrugged indifferently and walked in without me I would I have collapsed. But I guess an empty gut makes a convincing actor of a man. As I had hoped, he picked up his cue like a trouper.

"Oh, if it's the money, don't worry about paying for it. This time it's on me."

"Well, that's white of you, mister... er..." I didn't want to go on calling him just plain "sir." It sounded funny.

"Haskell is the name. But think nothing of it. When you make your first million you can do the same for me." He came out with one of those loud and sudden laughs of his evidently pleased that he had said something funny. I laughed with him because it was expected of me, but it wasn't such a hot joke. It is very easy to kid about dough—when you've got it.

"Well, much obliged, Mister Haskell damned lucky I met you. My name is Alexander Roth."

We sort of hesitated around, not knowing whether we ought to shake hands or what; then finally we did, awkwardly, and went into the restaurant. The smell of the place weakened me. It was a little chophouse with one of those open kitchens where a large black cook was barbecuing some meat. I could practically taste the stuff from thirty feet away. They had the joint fixed up sweet, and as soon as we walked in I could tell they clipped you plenty. When there are tablecloths and thin dishes in a roadhouse you can bet your life coffee's a dime. A waiter in a starched white mess-jacket gave me the once over as the screen door slammed behind us and I have an idea he would have tossed me out on my ear if he hadn't spotted Haskell. Even so, he gave me a dirty look, making me fed ill at ease. The way I was dressed, I should have been coming around the back, holding out my hand. "Two? This way, please."

The waiter was giving Haskell that prop smile of his and me the death's-head grin. Those bastards are all alike, the world over. I've worked in enough clubs and restaurants to know the breed backwards. They'll do anything for a tip, and they can smell where it's coming from a mile away. Anyhow, this guy certainly could. I didn't know him, but I hated him.

He showed us into a booth and I didn't waste any time sitting down and grabbing the menu. Have you ever been so hungry that you get to gnawing through the inside of your cheek? My mouth was full of canker sores.

"Don't you think we'd better wash before ordering?"

I looked up at Mr. Haskell and then down again in shame.

We were alone in the place—it being an odd time—but his voice sounded loud enough to be heard out in the street.

Besides, to add to my embarrassment, there was that grinning baboon with the napkin over his arm standing by the table. I felt like crawling into a hole somewhere. I knew I was dirty as hell. I hadn't had a bath in nine days; my hands were cracked and dusty and my nails were a sight. Jeez, if my old violin teacher, Professor Puglesi, could have seen those nails he would have dropped dead. He used to tell me that some day my hands would be my fortune. What a laugh! The old fellow meant all right I guess; however, on this trip, by far the most valuable finger on my hand was my thumb.

I shoved back the table and hopped out of the booth. "Sure, if you'd rather, Mr. Haskell. Only I thought it save a little time if we ordered now and then washed while he was getting it."

Haskell nodded. I knew I'd scored. "Maybe you're right at that, Detroit. I want to make Los Angeles before Saturday, so you see every minute counts."

"Yes, sir."

"I've got a line on a plug that runs back east at Belmont Park. It means dough to me if I can get in town before the race."

I yessed him again. What was he telling me all this

for? He didn't want to get there any quicker than I did. It seemed like years since last I saw Sue. In all that time I'd been living the life of a monk.... Well, practically the life of monk. Sue told me before she left that she didn't expect me to be faithful to her—although she, naturally, would be faithful to me. "Men aren't built that way," she said, "and as long as it doesn't mean anything, I don't really mind. So go out when you feel like it and have a good time." I thought that was very broad minded of her, yet somehow, I didn't like it. I wanted her to want me to be faithful—even if I wasn't.

Haskell was looking at the menu. "How about a steak, Detroit?"

Imagine! A steak!

"Do you mean it?" I stammered. The guy didn't sound like a ribber.

"Why not? That's what I'm having."

Then and there I decided this fellow was tops. Feature it. He not only lifts me for hundreds of miles, he buys me steak dinners! And to think that a couple of minutes before I'd been reading the menu from right to left. I didn't know the proper thing to say to him, so I didn't say anything.

"Two sirloin steak dinners," he told the grinning duck at his elbow. "And be sure you make them rare."

"Yes, sir. Very good, sir."

I liked mine well done, but I let it go at that.

It was while I was scrubbing the thick layer of road-dust from my face and hands that I first took a good look at this angel of mine. You know how it is. When you're strictly on your rear-end you kind of feel inferior; you don't look a guy over to size him up when he's giving you a break. You feel thankful enough to be getting the break. Haskell was behind me, looking into the wall-mirror over my shoulder while he combed his hair. He had a rather a handsome face, only it looked a little bloated, as if he'd been keeping late hours or something. It was tanned from the sun, but even so it had the

appearance of pallor, a certain puffiness under his eyes
and around the corners of his mouth. The eyes
themselves were brown like mine, only they were
bloodshot and tired and the pupils looked dilated a
little—caused by driving too much, no doubt. He was
about my own height and build, but probably three or
four years my senior. The thing that struck me funny,
though, was his nose. It was almost the duplicate of my
own. His had the same kind of bump at the bridge which
sort of threw the nose a little to one side. And the nostrils
flared, too. He must have seen me staring at it, because
he asked what was up. I told him.

"You think we look alike?" He frowned a little into
the glass.

"Oh, I don't know. I can't see a resemblance."

"Well," I insisted, "you're older than me, for one
thing. But take a look at my nose. See, that bump there?
I broke it, riding the tail-board of an ice-wagon when I
was ten. You've got that kind of a bump, too.

"He laughed at that. "I assure you, bud, I was never
on an ice-wagon in my life."

"No, but you've got that bump. I'll grant you we don't
look like brothers, but..."

"Well, you can have the job of posing for all my
passport photographs. How about that?"

"No, but seriously, Mr. Haskell, don't you think—"

"I can't see it," he cut in, getting tired of the
conversation. "If you're ready, let's get going."

I shut up pronto. He was just in a hurry, not sore.
Nevertheless, I wouldn't have blamed him much if he had
been sore. I looked like the wrath of God. When I left New
York I wasn't wearing the proper clothing for a trip of this
kind; and noticing the expensive grey tweeds he had on, I
became all the more conscious of my sweaty, dollar polo
shirt and my ragged pants. Well, maybe we didn't look
much alike.

He did most of the talking during the rest of the hour
we were in the cafe. I ate. He rambled on about his family

who lived in Bel-Air, his kid sister he had always been so crazy about, his mother who had died the year before he ran away, his father whom he had always despised, and stuff like that. Every now and then I'd come out with a "Yes?" or an "Is that so?" but I wasn't paying much attention. That steak kept me busy. It was a little tough—I guess it wasn't cooked enough—but need I mention I enjoyed it? It tasted like the manna must have tasted to the starving Jews wandering around in the wilderness for God knows how long. I began to feel myself again with that under my belt, and the morbid pictures I'd been conjuring up in my mind for weeks suddenly went like Margaret Mitchell's book. By the time the dessert came I was in such a pleasant frame of mind that even the thought of Sue out there alone among the Hollywood wolves did not bother me.

And, believe you me, that's saying something. Sue was—and for that matter must still be—a gal who can bother anybody under the age of seventy. Pretty as a dream, blonde and green-eyed, it is her habit to open those big eyes wide, pout that red Cupid mouth, and crawl right in under a guy's skin. That is exactly the way she crawled in under mine. But once she's there she festers and it takes plenty of time and liquor to get her out of your system. One fellow I know back in New York stayed in love with her for months after she handed him his hat. He used to walk around in a fog and get drunk every night. Once he even tried to commit suicide. That's the way Sue affects people. But let me tell you how I happened to get mixed up with her. I know it's the old story, but I like to think about it.

I met her while I was playing first fiddle in a little club on West 57th Street, not far from Columbus Circle. I was only doing that sort of work to force my old man off the relief rolls. He wanted me to go on studying under Professor Puglesi; but I'm funny that way. I don't like people making any sacrifices for me—not even my own father. As it was, my dad almost died of shame when I came home one day and told him what I was doing and that I intended to keep it up. And the professor? Well, he damned near blew his cork.

"A concert violinist playing jazz music in a cheap night club! Ye gods! My boy, in three—maybe even two—years I will have you making your debut. You will be the envy of everybody who can call himself a musician. Believe what I am telling you and quit this foolish job right away."

And nothing he could say would change my mind. I told myself that if I really had something on the ball it would come out no matter what I did. Besides, how did I know I was as good as I was cracked up to be? I had only the professor's word for it, and maybe he was dishing out a lot of hot air so he could keep getting that two bucks a lesson.

Anyway, that's how I fell in with Sue. Only don't get the idea she was one of the club's headliners or plugged songs or sold cigarettes. She was just one of the fifteen-dollar-a-week cuties in the floor-show chorus. She was great on looks, but the dance-director used to complain to Bellman that she had two left legs. That may or may not have been true, but to me she stood out like nobody's business, making the rest of the girls look sick and sixty. Her hair was about the color of polished brass, with that same metallic shine to it; and it fell down to her shoulders, and it was straight except for the ends, which she kept curled under. It formed a perfect frame for that delicate nose and those enormous dark green eyes. But if her face and hair were lovely, her body was something special. She was of slight build, with a waist so slender every time she bent over you expected her to break. I won't go into all the details, but engineers ought to go to her for lessons in streamlining. With her looks she didn't have to know how to dance.

It took me all of three weeks to gather up enough nerve to ask her for a date. When finally I did she said she had a date; however, the following night she let me

take her home on the Fifth Avenue bus that runs up
Riverside. It was quite a long ride—she lived uptown near
Seaman Avenue and Dyckman Street—but in all the time
it took us to get there I don't think I said ten words to
her. She had me completely buffaloed, and before the
bus passed 72nd Street I was in love with her. I could
feel her little body against my arm and the perfume she
had on was enough to make any man bite through a bar
of cast-iron. It was heaven, let me tell you. I guess she
must have realized how I felt, because when we reached
her door she kissed me good night and said I was sweet
and good night again, she'd see me tomorrow; then she
kissed me again. I rode home on the downtown subway
that night and passed my stop.

All this was about three months after my father died.
I was still feeling pretty low about it and the apartment
seemed awfully dark and empty without him. His old
Morris-chair continued to stand by the living-room
window where he used to sit by the hour and stare down
into the street. Right after the funeral I packed everything
of his away and stored it in the basement because I
didn't want to think about him any more. It only made
me feel rotten. But now and then I'd run across one of
his pipes or something and I'd go soft as mush. For that
reason I stayed away from home as much as possible. I
would have moved in a minute if the landlord would have
let me break the lease.

One night Sue and I got to drinking after the club
closed and we wound up only a few blocks from where I
lived. I took her up there, and to my astonishment she
said she'd appreciate it if I let her stay all night. She
explained she was tight and couldn't face her mother in
that condition. She didn't look that tight to me, but you
can bet your sweet life I didn't send her home. We slept
together for the first time that night and after that we
went to my house a lot.

I was truly overboard by then. However, don't be
misled and think it was one of those sexual attachments

story-writers are always talking about. Of course I enjoyed staying with her, but there was something else, too. Words can't describe it, but if you've ever been in love you'll know what I mean.

There were times when I wanted to hold her off at a distance so mat I could see her and appreciate her without my emotions being hammered to pieces; and then at other times I couldn't get close enough. I'd imagine there was a wall between us and I'd try my damnedest to break through. I felt that I was outside, and that wasn't enough. Sometimes I'd lay awake at night fighting the desire to reach out and turn on the bed-lamp so I could look at her. Once I did turn it on. It woke Sue up and she got sore, so I never tried it again. But I wanted to. Do you get what I mean? If you don't, it's the best I can do.

Then one day her mother found out about us. Don't ask me how. I haven't the faintest idea unless Sue talked in her sleep or kept a diary. Being one of the straitlaced kind—the kind of woman who wears a corset under her nightgown—she told her daughter to get out and stay out. She wasn't fooling, either. I went around and tried to argue with Mrs. Harvey, but it was no soap. When I explained that my intentions were honorable, that I loved her daughter and intended to marry her just as soon as I earned a little more money, she slammed the door in my face. So there remained nothing else but for Sue to move in with me, which she did, bag and baggage. We got along beautifully, Sue and I. True, she wasn't much of a housekeeper—being more the bohemian type—and most of the time it was I who had to do the cleaning; but she made up for that in other ways. Just her presence in that small, dreary apartment was enough to compensate for what the neighbors must have thought. Oh, they believed we were married all right; but one day they caught a glimpse of our place. They must have thought we lived like pigs. Well, we did, I suppose. What's a little dust and a few dirty dishes when you're in love?

During this period I don't think I missed a day without asking her to marry me and make it permanent. I'd start in on it in the morning after breakfast, at lunch, at dinner between numbers at the club and in bed at night. Sue insisted she was every bit as much in love as I was, but that marriage is a serious step and people should never go into a thing like that until they were sure. I was sure all right; maybe she wasn't. Nevertheless, with all the cold water she threw on the idea, one night, after we had been living together for almost three months, she agreed to be the Mrs.

"I'm only doing it so that I can have a little peace," she laughed. I laughed too when I wondered which way to take that.

It was early in the spring when I got fired for poking a customer in the jaw. I'm usually a very quiet guy, and I don't pick fights unless they're forced on me; but there were a lot of wiseacres who came into the Break O'Dawn stag, looking for whatever they could pick up. This one bird made a pass at Sue while she was on the floor doing her number. It wasn't much, really—all he did was pat her fanny—but it riled me, I saw red, hopped off the bandstand and let him have it. The management put him out, and when work was over Bellman came up and told me I was through. I expected him at least to give me two weeks' pay. All I got was the curl of his lip. That, naturally, was grounds for a beef to the Union. However, I didn't want to make trouble on account of Sue.

I was sorry to lose that job; not that the money was much, but because it meant not being able to work with her. As things turned out, though, it wouldn't have made much difference. Less than a month later she decided to go to Hollywood, on spec. A friend of hers kept writing that she was doing fine out there and how marvelous the sunshine was and how it never rained in Southern California; that was all the encouragement Sue needed.

"But we were supposed to get married next Monday!" I howled.

"We'll get married when I come back, Alex, huh? Or when you come out. Say, that's an idea. Why don't you come out, too?"

She knew very well why I couldn't come out. I had fourteen bucks left in the bank. So all I could do was kiss her good-bye and tell her to be sure to write at least once a week. She did, about a month later, enclosing a ten-dollar bill, which she said she was sure I could use. It came in very handy. She must have been a mind reader or psychic or something, because I just couldn't find work. No band seemed to be short on fiddles. I made the rounds six days a week, but summer is a bad season for everything in New York. Then one day I went to see a friend of mine who is an assistant program director at N.B.C. and he advised me to sleep mornings. I put the bee on him for twenty bucks and decided to follow Sue.

In a way, her leaving wasn't so bad, and I began to feel much better about things. It gave me an excuse to do what I'd always dreamed of doing: striking out to the west. When we were kids it was the Indians we wanted to hunt; now it's the movies. I know I'm probably the millionth guy to start out for the film capital, hoping to connect; but why shouldn't I be able to crash the racket? I'm not Heifetz or Kreisler, but I can handle a bow a lot better than Rubinoff, for instance, and I'm only twenty-nine and not bad looking. The only cockeyed feature about me is my nose, and that shouldn't prove such a handicap. I understand they can hook enough filters, portrait-attachments and jiggers to the camera to make Madame X look like Shirley Temple.

My only regret in starting for L.A. was my fiddle. Since the only way I could afford to cross the country was to bum it, I didn't need train or bus fare. But I'd have to eat, so into hock it went—along with the few pieces of furniture that were paid for, two suits and my working tux. That stuff I didn't mind pawning, but I'd need the violin to work. It was no Stradivarius, I'll grant you, but it could carry a tune with the best of them. As the professor always claimed, a true artist doesn't need an expensive instrument. He can get by with an old cigar-box and a couple of yards of cat-gut.

The going wasn't so bad in the east. I didn't have any trouble catching rides—except around Philadelphia, where you can catch about everything else—and all went along smoothly until I ran into tough luck in Dallas. My money was all gone and I was thrown in the jug for swiping some fruit off a stand. I'm no thief, but, boy, three days of penny candy can make a great difference in a fellow's scruples. The cops treated me mean, slapped me around plenty, took my picture and finger-prints; then they hauled me into court. When he heard the charges against me the judge smiled kind of wistfully. He was a benign sort, that judge; he looked like an owl, with his bald head and heavy spectacles.

"Another State v. Jean Valjean, eh?"

Maybe he had a notion I didn't know what he was talking about, but I'd seen that picture, too. The arresting officer evidently hadn't. "You must have the wrong case, Your Honor. This man is Alexander Roth."

The judge didn't say anything for a moment, just sat there on the bench, peering at me through those milk-bottle lenses. Then he sighed wearily. "Thirty days," he said. "When you get out, Roth, come back and see me. Next case."

I thought it was a bum rap, but when I went back to see him he wrote me a letter of reference. That was nice of him, especially since he didn't mention that I'd served time. In the letter he called me a personal friend of his, I still had the thing in my valise.

The guy across the table from me was just finishing his dessert. I'd finished mine ten minutes before, He took a final slug of coffee and then wiped his lips with a napkin. As if that was some prearranged signal, the waiter approached, still wearing that sickly smile, and laid the check on the table, face down. I've often wondered why waiters do that. Is it because they don't want to spoil the customer's appetite?

"All set, Detroit?"

"Yes, sir. That certainly was grand of you to..."

"Forget it—forget it."

"Oh, I can't do that. I'll bet there's not another man who'd have—"

He shut me up with a wave of the hand and, reaching into his inside pocket, took out a big black wallet. My heart almost stopped beating when I got a flash of that thick sheaf of twenties and tens. I'd never before seen a roll like that one, not even in the clubs. The sight of so much cash really got me, and I scarcely breathed while he was thumbing through it. I tried to look away—because I was afraid if he saw me watching him he might think I was getting ideas—but I just couldn't remove my eyes.

They say that money is nothing, that a buck is only a piece of paper crawling with germs, and that you can't buy happiness with cash. I say sour grapes. Name me one thing money can't buy. Respect? That's usually the first item people mention. Well, will you tell me who respects a guy without money? A guy that's starving, say, or on the bum? Go on the bum some time and find out how much respect you get. I know. Love? That's usually the next come-back. Brother, don't ever let anyone pull that one on you. You can win a woman a lot easier with a mink coat than with poetry and walks in the park. But what got me off on this?

The check couldn't have been more than two and a half, but Haskell paid it with a fin.

"Keep the change, Mac," he told the waiter. I made up my mind that I must be riding with some kind of crook. No honest man would think of tipping a waiter like that.

The road from Lordsburg to Phoenix—U.S. 70—winds around an awful lot through mountain passes. The scenery is really beautiful, if you like mat sort of thing. I don't. Wilderness may be O.K. for animals and hermits, but give me cultivated lawns, buildings and people every time. When I was a young sprout I had an ambition to become a cowboy and roam the range, shooting rustlers and rescuing good-looking women. But I'm older and wiser now and I've learned there are more good-looking numbers to be had by riding around in a flashy car with a pocketful of chips.

While we were tearing around curves the sun was going down. The sky became a dull red, gradually growing darker as if it was cooling off which, as a matter of fact, it was. Somehow I wasn't at all nervous any more and I didn't keep wondering what would happen if we blew a tire or met a truck on a bend. I just leaned back, completely at ease puffing away on the cigar Haskell treated me to. If we had run off a cliff then, I'd have died feeling happy. Funny how little it actually takes to make a man contended. Why, if it had been Sue there alongside me, there would have been nothing more I could ask of the world.

Haskell was driving without his sunglasses and I noticed that his eyes looked sleepy. He was squinting a little and the lids drooped. The puffiness in his face had gone away, only now there were bags and pouches and his skin had a transparency about it. I could almost see clean through to his cheek-bones. The man looked unhealthy. "Want me to take over for a while, Mr. Haskell?"

He thought it over for a few seconds. "Well... think you can handle her all right?"

"Sure. I'll take it easy. You must be all fagged out, driving so long."

Haskell covered a yawn. "I am, rather. Didn't get much sleep last night in El Paso. All right, Detroit. Wait until we come to the next gas station. Tank's almost empty, anyway."

We swung into a Shell joint about twenty minutes later and two attendants rushed out, smiling the company smile—from ear to ear. An independent dealer will smile according to the amount of gas you buy, but these college graduates, most of them engineers, lawyers, bacteriologists, BA. and B.S. men cum laude, cheerfully wipe your windshield, put water in your radiator, check the headlights and battery, add air, clean the steering-wheel, and do everything else they can think of but give you a shave and a shine. Haskell broke out his roll again and handed me a twenty. It was definitely a thrill. I hadn't had that much dough in my hands for months.

"Tell them to fill her up and change the oil. I'm going in the back. Hey, Johnny," he called to one of the attendants, "where is it?"

"You have to go out there to the shed, mister."

"I hate this natural plumbing," he said to me.

"I won't be long."

When he came back I handed him his change. He counted it. "Let me see. You're giving me back sixteen twenty-two. That leaves three seventy-eight. That must have been twelve gallons at nineteen and six quarts at two-bits. Correct isn't it?" My jaw dropped wide open. Jimmy, this guy certainly was up on his arithmetic! What was he, anyway? A. C.P.A.? I knocked wood mentally that I hadn't tried to pocket a few dimes on the transaction.

He smiled when he saw the look on my face.

"Yes, I'm pretty good at figures, Detroit. I should be. I wrote sheet for seven years."

That explained it. He was a bookie.

When we got going again, with me at the wheel, Haskell rode with his head resting against the back of the seat and his eyes closed. I hit a steady pace of fifty-five, which I decided was plenty in the dark with all those twists and turns. Not only that, it was getting a little foggy, and the headlights of approaching cars, even after they were dimmed, blinded me. Half the time I didn't even bother to strain my eyes to see ahead; I merely followed the line in the center of the road. After about an hour passed, and Haskell still rode in that same position, I thought he may be asleep. It startled me when he suddenly said, "Hey Detroit, have you got a stick of gum on you, by any chance?"

"I'm sorry, Mr. Haskell, I haven't."

"My mouth feels so dry," he grunted, shifting his position an inch or so. "Guess my stomach is upset a little. No wonder, with all these lousy restaurant meals."

"A shot of bi-car ought to fix you up, Mr. Haskell. What's the trouble? Didn't that steak go down right?"

"Oh, I don't know. I've been feeling this way all afternoon. My tongue feels like a wad of paper. And water doesn't seem to do much good I've had gallons."

"How ill do you feel?" I asked, not that I gave a damn.

"Eh? Oh, I guess I'm all right."

"Want to stop and see a doctor at the next town?"

"Hell, no," he grumbled. "It's not that bad. I guess I can wait until we get to Los Angeles. We should be there tomorrow afternoon—or tomorrow night if we stop over some place. The trouble is there's no place of any size to stop at between here and the coast, except Phoenix. We ought to be in there pretty soon."

"In about an hour, I guess. You want me to stop when we hit Phoenix?"

"No. Keep going."

"O.K."

That suited me down to the ground. If he decided to stop over somewhere, I could count on a night spent walking around or sleeping in the car.

"But if you pass a drug store anywhere along the line, stop. I want to buy some gum and put more iodine on these scratches. They sting like hell. There ought to be a law against women with sharp nails."

I felt like saying that was what he got for playing around. However, I had sense enough to keep my mouth shut. What business was it of mine if he tried to manhandle some dame?

"I know how you must feel," I remarked sympathetically. "I've been scratched like that lots of times myself. One time the gal I was sleeping with got so passionate she damned near ripped my back to pieces."

Another of my lies. Nothing like that had ever happened to me. I hear women do get like that now and then; but never one that I had out. It sounded good, though.

"Well, it's the first time for me. And the last. God, females are unreasonable! One minute they love you and the next they're ready to tear your face to ribbons. Well, no woman can do that to me and expect me to forgive her. I put her out on her ear."

"That's the stuff," I said.

"I don't believe in babying them, like some men do. If they get out of line, slap them down. They'll respect you for it in the long run." He paused and yawned. "Say, open that glove compartment and get out my cigarette-case, will you?"

I felt around in there until I pulled out the long, silver case, thin as a dime.

"Want me to light one for you, Mr. Haskell?"

He opened his eyes in a jiffy. "No, no. That's all right. I'll light it myself."

He lit it and by the flare of the match I saw that his hands were trembling, although the night air was warm as toast. I figured he must have some sort of fever. I began praying he wouldn't ask me to put up the top and roll up the windows because I can't stand the smell of Egyptian tobacco. I don't mind it when I'm smoking it, understand; but when I'm not, it gets me in the stomach. A few drags on the cigarette, however, seemed to stop him shivering. He sat up.

"Turn on the radio, Detroit. Let's have some music. Then maybe I'll forget I'm broke."

Broke? Broke my grandmother. What was this? Another one of his lousy gags?

"I should be as broke as you are," I said, trying to get a laugh into my voice, "every day in the week." I turned the radio knob disgustedly and fiddled with the station selector.

"Eh?" He looked round at me with that sleepy, amused expression an Englishman always has on his face when he's making love. "Oh, you mean the two-three dollars I've got on me? Say, that's no dough. Do you know what's happened to me? They took me. Cleaned me like a Long Island duck. One race—thirty-eight grand. Can you imagine?"

I couldn't. As soon as any mentioned amount got above a dollar forty cents it was out of my line entirely.

"And I was supposed to be the know-it-all! Why, I can't even raise another stake—and after ten years on the track. They closed my book down as if I'd only opened yesterday with a two-bit roll."

"That's a shame," I said, really feeling a little sorry for the guy.

"A shame? It's a laugh, that's what it is." Then he began to curse—and, boy, what a vocabulary! He goddamned his sheet-writer, the Racing Secretary, the Commissioner, the handicappers, the horses themselves and a whole string of people I never heard of. He raved on for a couple of minutes; yet he didn't seem really angry.

The radio warmed up. Some announcer was plugging a salad-dressing. I gave him the hook and caught a weather forecast. We were due for some rain. By this time Haskell had smoked his cigarette almost down to his first knuckle. He took one final drag and then clinched it and put it back inside the case. That struck me funny. With all the heavy sugar he was packing, he was saving stumps like any tramp. There was something mighty screwy about this Mr. Haskell.

"But I'll dig up another stake, Detroit—see if I don't. I'll be back when the season opens in Miami with fresh dough, plenty of it, and no tightwad backers to worry about, either."

"That's the spirit."

"Just watch," he yawned.

"Sure you will. Never say die, brother," was my

damned-fool comment. I was humoring him like a drunk.

As we rode along Haskell was smiling with his eyes closed. He seemed to derive huge satisfaction from thinking about the secret supply he was aiming to tap. Well, I was way ahead of him. From what he had been telling me about his family at the dinner-table I could read his mind. Everywhere his old man went his footprints were dollar-signs.

I finally got some orchestra on KATAR, Phoenix. The violin section was terrible.

I drove all that night while Haskell slept like a log. The only time he moved a muscle was when the car hit a few bumps the other side of Phoenix. But every now and then he'd start to snore and I'd remember he was there. He'd make his mouth move, too—twitch his jaw and move his tongue around to moisten his lips. And once in a while he'd mutter something in his sleep. I didn't like it. It sent prickles up my spine. After about two hours I began to grow sleepy myself. I hadn't had a decent night's rest since I got out of the Dallas jail. My eyelids started drooping and a couple of times I had to shake my head to wake myself up.

I would be handing you a lot of Abe Lincoln baloney if I said I wasn't tempted once or twice during the night to slug Mr. Haskell over the head and roll him for his cash. So I won't say it. The guy was treating me right and I couldn't bring myself to the point of hurting him. It took plenty of self-control, though. Remember, I was desperately in need of money; and in the glove-compartment of the car was a small Stillson wrench and a pair of heavy driving-gloves I could have used for padding. It was a cinch set-up if ever there was one.

I realize all this sounds bad. But try to get me straight. I'm a musician, not a thug. The few dishonorable things I did I didn't want to do—I had to do. Anyway, this is one of the things I passed up—and I'm not asking you to pin a merit-badge on me, either. The only boy Scout rule I ever followed was: "Be Prepared".

I didn't do much thinking that night while I was rolling along. It was too hazy, and a wandering mind at the wheel of a car in a fog spells bad news. Besides, all there was to think of was Los Angeles and what I was going to do when I got there. I'd been thinking of that for weeks. My plans, as usual, were a little vague. I was counting on Sue being able to advance me a little dough—just enough to keep me for a week or so until I found work. According to a friend of mine, musicians never starve in Hollywood. There are plenty of dance bands around, dozens of little cocktail joints where, in a pinch, a fellow could play solo for tips, and then, of course, there are the studios. There are always dubbing jobs to be had and scenes where the hero is supposed to walk off a cliff or out of a second-story window playing a violin. That's where I came in. I'm laughing. Since Sue was not expecting me, and since she was staying with a girl friend, I'd have to bunk some place else. But that didn't worry me. I generally manage to get by.

About a hundred miles west of Phoenix and seventy east of Blythe dawn began to break. I could see it coming in the rear-view mirror: first a grey strip on the black, then a blue tinge, and then a kind of reddish brown. Ahead of me it was still dark and foggy; behind it was fast becoming clear. That's a mighty lonesome stretch of desert in there. On either side of the road are deep black gullies, some of them twenty and thirty feet down. If you've got any sort of an imagination, driving alone through there is liable to get you. It's dry as a bone in that section during the summer and every now and then the State Department or some motor club leaves a rain-barrel on the shoulder of the road in case a motorist's radiator leaks. In the gloom they look like little hitch-hikers. At that time of day the whole countryside has a ghostly quality, about it. Shadows shift along the ground as your car climbs and descends little hills, leaving portions of the highway light and other parts pitch dark. A couple of times I jammed on the brakes because I imagined something or somebody was crossing the road. They tell me that most of the accidents in those hills take place about dawn or dusk. The gas gauge showed almost empty, but I thought I'd better let Haskell sleep until we hit a service station.

Waking him then wouldn't have done any good. To tell the truth, the look of the road got me a little panicky. The last station I passed was a good eight miles back, and this stretch didn't even have billboards. I knew Haskell would sure as hell hand me my walking papers if we ran out in the middle of nowhere, so I drove with my fingers crossed.

It was about that time that the haze turned into rain. A fine drizzle began to cloud the windshield and I had to switch on the wipers. A few miles of this and my clothes felt damp and uncomfortable. I decided that before it started to pour we'd better put up the top.

I nudged Haskell. "It's beginning to rain, Mr. Haskell."

Not a peep out of him.

I pushed him again, this time harder. Then I shook him a little. "It's beginning to rain, Mr. Haskell. Shall I put up the top?"

When I couldn't even get a rise out of him I made up my mind to keep going until either we hit a gas station or ran out. I knew it would be practically impossible to get the top up without waking him.

Since the guy was so dead to the world I thought it wouldn't hurt if I sneaked one of his smokes. I'm a tobacco fiend if ever there was one, and all I'd had that day was one cigar. If Haskell woke up and caught me, it was such a little thing he couldn't very well get sore. I could tell him that I was falling asleep and smoking kept me awake. That settled, I opened the glove-compartment as quietly as possible, found the case and helped myself to a butt. I didn't have a match, but—miracles will never cease—the dashboard lighter worked. While I was doing this the rain really began to beat down hard. The drops hit the leather upholstery of the back and rolled on to the seats. My pants felt sticky. I don't think I took more than four or five puffs on the cigarette before I started to get dizzy. After every drag it got worse. The road commenced to bank and turn and whirl in the windshield. The wipers seemed to be working at twice their normal speed. Inside of me I felt a sudden tightening, as if my intestines had tied themselves into a knot around my stomach. Luckily, as the cigarette slipped from between my fingers, I was not too far gone to have the presence of mind to apply brakes. The car skidded, swung around crazily and then stopped.

My head felt light as a feather and I had the curious sensation of floating about. Of course I knew at once what was the matter. The reason Mr. Haskell was clinching his butts was because they were reefers, sticks of jive. The guy was a tea-hound. I'd only tried smoking marihuana once before, but there could be no mistaking that balmy, sickish sensation which distorts everything and makes a marble look like a basket-ball.

The car began to roll backward down a slope. I yanked the emergency and, leaning well over the door, got sick all over the road. The coyotes got the first steak I'd had in my belly for nearly three months.

I heaved all there was to heave and in a few minutes I felt better. My temples were still throbbing but the dizziness was gone. Looking over, I saw that Haskell had not moved during all this. He was still slumped against the far door, the raindrops hitting his forehead and rolling down his face. I knew that if that didn't wake him, no shaking in the world would. The bastard must be high as a kite on that weed.

I cut the motor.

Putting up a wet top is no cinch, and I had to struggle with it. I got my side straightened out all right, but there was nothing I could do to the other without opening the door on Haskell's side of the car and kneeling on the seat. By that time the rain was letting up a bit. Nevertheless, as the clothes I had on were the only things I owned, I made up my mind that—Haskell or no Haskell—the top was going up. Holding my splitting head with one hand, I walked around to his side of the car and jerked open the door.

All right. Now you've reached the part where all the mess beings. You'll probably take the rest of the story with a grain of salt or maybe just come right out and call me seven different brands of liar. It sounds fishy—but I can't help that, any more than I could have helped what happened. Up to then I did things my way; but from then on something else stepped in and shunted me off to a different destination than the one I had planned for myself. And there was nothing in the world I could do to prevent it. The things I did were the only things left open for me to do. I had to take and like whatever came along.

For when I pulled open that door, Mr. Haskell fell and cracked his skull on the running-board. He went out like a light.

Isn't that a laugh? Can't you just picture the fellow with horns laughing like a son of a bitch and slapping his knee? Sure it's funny. If Haskell came to, even he would swear I conked him with a wrench for his dough!

But here's something funnier. He never came to. As soon as I dragged his legs out of the car and propped him up against one of the fenders, I saw he was dead. His face was a yellowish color, except for the long purple bruise extending across his forehead where he'd connected with the running-board. He looked ghastly. That's the only word for it.

I guess I went nuts there for a minute. I slapped his face as hard as I could and called him by name; I rubbed his wrists and shook him until his teeth rattled. No dice. He wasn't breathing and there was no pulse at all. He may have been dead before he cracked his skull, I don't know. But one thing was sure: the man was worm bait.

Can you appreciate what a nice pickle it was? There was I, a vagrant; and there he was, a rich race-track sport with all kinds of dough, a swanky car and a cracked head. Who but a moron would believe me when I said he fell out of the car? Some cops are pretty dumb, I'll grant you; but not one of them, not the greenest rookie in New York, would fall for a story like that. To make matters worse, I was just out of jail for petty larceny in Dallas. What if I did only grab a bunch of bananas and run? What that guy had in his pocket would buy plenty of bananas.

It looked very much like I was in for it. Any judge and any jury in the world would have yelled "Murder in the First Degree" at the top of his lungs. I began to wonder what sort of execution the State of Arizona provided—hanging or lethal gas. Then a flash of Sue's face hit me hard. I'd never see her again. She would believe I hadn't done it all right... but, probably, she was the only person who would.

I was wet clean through: my shirt and pants from the rain, my body from sweat. Kidding aside, I was never so frightened in all my life. I was so scared I couldn't think, and I knew I had to do something. What? You tell me. The first thing off the bat, I guess a person's instinct makes him want to run, and to run like hell. That's the way I wanted to run, but I had sense enough to realize I couldn't get very far before the law caught up with me. I stifled the urge by reminding myself that there were several people back down the highway who could identify me. There was that heel waiter in the restaurant at Lordsburg, and the cook, and the two attendants in the filling station. I would really be in a sweet spot then, trying to explain to the cops why I took it on the Arthur Duffy. Running for it is a sure sign of a guilty conscience. The next possibility was to sit tight and tell the truth when the cops came. That would be crazy. That wouldn't be Daniel going into the lions' den; that would be Daniel

going into the lions' den at feeding-time, eating a
hamburger. Hell, before I'd do that I'd run.

But standing alongside a car in the middle of the
road with a dead man propped up against a fender was
just asking for trouble. If somebody passed by it would
be all over but the hanging, or gassing, or whatever it
might be. I'm pretty strong, but it was no easy job
dragging Mr. Haskell back into his seat and slamming
the door. Not only was he heavy, but I didn't want to
touch him. It gave me a funny feeling I didn't like. Well,
like it or not, it had to be done. I got him up there and
then I went round the car and climbed in under the
wheel. I was completely fagged out. My knees felt like
water and my head ached terribly. I just sat there in the
car for it must have been ten minutes, panting like the
dickens, my teeth chattering as if it was cold. I kept
moaning, "Why did you have to die now? Why did you
have to die now?" I tried to stop, but I couldn't.

Finally I heard the sound of a car coming towards
me from the west. That snapped me out of it in a hurry. I
started up the motor and got the Buick moving. It jerked
around and almost stalled because my foot was shaking
on the clutch pedal, but once I was in high it was O.K.
Instinctively I realized that I was safe as long as I was on
the highway and moving, but I also realized that I
couldn't drive more than a few miles without stopping to
take on gas. The gauge read empty. If I ran out... well,
that would be curtains.

The other car came on full blast and flashed by like a
bat out of hell. I'm sure he was going too fast to notice
whether there were two of us in the Buick or just one. I
breathed a little easier. One danger was past.

When my head cleared a bit, and I was getting over
my first shock and panic, I reasoned that the
circumstances pointed to but to one escape: if I was to
get away, I would have to get rid of the body immediately.
Alone I had a chance, but carting a stiff around in an
open car was the same as shaking hands with the

warden. Having come to that conclusion, I swung off on to the shoulder of the road and locked the ignition. I stood up on the seat so that I could look down into the gully. It was only nine or ten feet deep in there, but thick with underbrush. Obviously an ideal place. If I hid him carefully, nobody should run across him for a long time.

I listened for a few minutes before doing anything. When I was sure no car was coming I hopped out, ran round and hauled Haskell onto the shoulder near the edge of the ravine. I got him on the brink, laid him down parallel with the road and then gave him a shove. He rolled down, crashing through the bushes, until I heard him hit the bottom. He must have landed on his head, because it wasn't a dull thud like you read about in books. It was a very sharp sound, something like a cue striking a billiard-ball, only with more of a ring to it than that and with a cracking.... Well anyway it was horrible.

I'll never forget it.

I waited and listened a little while before I slid down after him. My plan was to cover him with brush, not to rob him. Nevertheless, as my mind began to function properly I remembered the car. That would be brilliant, wouldn't it? There are deserted Buicks all along the highway! So there you are. Any dope can see that there was nothing else to do but take the car with me. Leaving it there would be like erecting a tombstone.

That is the way it began, and, as the book says, one thing leads to another. I knew that even if I drove the car for only a hundred miles or so, and then deserted it, I would need money for gas and oil. Anyway, it was stupid to think of leaving all that dough on a man who was dead. I helped myself to his money.

I was about to place the wallet back in his pocket when I remembered that I'd better have the registration to the car and his driver's license, too—in case somebody stopped me. I was sure to get by with those. I could pass for thirty-two easily, and my hair and eyes corresponded with the description on the license. I stuffed the wallet into my pocket.

You see, by that time I'd done just what the police would think I'd done—even if I hadn't. It sounds punchy, but the only way I could beat the rap for something I didn't do was to do it. I had no choice in the matter. Oh, very well, if you want to get technical. I had the choice either of staying alive or committing suicide. Put it that way.

I was just getting ready to leave him and climb back on to the road when I thought of something else: the way I was dressed. Wearing the clothes I had on would not look kosher for the owner of such an expensive car. Some cop might pull me in on suspicion if I was stopped for some minor violation of traffic rules.

In the drizzle I yanked my clothes off. My nerves were so completely shot that I tore a big hole in the collar of my polo-shirt in trying to get it off without unbuttoning it all the way. I knew if anyone passed and stopped then it would be impossible to explain myself and the game would be up. The guy's shoes pinched somewhat because my feet were swollen, but his shirt was my size and his coat and trousers fitted fairly well. Everything but the coat was pretty dry because the heavy underbrush protected the gully. The only stitch I left on Mr. Haskell was his underwear. I'm finicky about such things.

After I dressed in his clothes, I put mine on him. They didn't look right, though. He was clean shaven, his hair was neatly trimmed and his nails manicured A crumby polo-shirt and an old pair of pants looked funny on a man like that. Yet somehow I couldn't laugh.

I covered him carefully with brush when I'd finished dressing him, but as I was about to climb the bank something else caught my eye. He had on a gold signet ring, a massive thing with his initials in what looked to me like platinum. It was tight and I had a tough time getting it off his stiff finger. Why did I take his ring? So they couldn't identify him, of course. If they just found a dead man dressed in those clothes they might figure it was only some bum who'd got into a fight. With that ring on him it would be different. Sure, and why should some crooked cop stick it into his pocket and have it melted down for somebody's maid? The thing looked like it might have a gold value of at least twenty bucks. I slipped the ring on my own finger, made sure Haskell was well covered, and climbed back out on to the road. By this time it was daylight. The sky was a dirty blue with rain clouds hanging low. There was no sign of the sun. I started for the car. Then I froze. All the strength in my body suddenly ebbed away and it was all I could do to keep on my feet.

Standing beside the car was a motor-cycle cop.

He was walking slowly around the car when I came up out of the gully. His machine was parked ten feet away with its headlight still burning, I could read what was written across the fuel-tank: Arizona State Highway Patrol. This was no messenger boy. He was checking the New York plates with some numbers he had in a little book, so it was a few seconds before he lifted his head and saw me.

"Oh, there you are," he said.

The blood was pumping through me like mad. I felt like running. But I didn't feel like getting shot. "Yes, here I am." It was a stupid answer, but I couldn't think. At that moment the world seemed to fade, numbing me upstairs. I think if he had asked me my name I wouldn't have been able to remember it. Sue and every other person I'd ever known would have been strangers to me if they had suddenly come along. The badge on the cop's cap was the only thing that registered.

"You the owner of this car?"

I opened my mouth to say I was but I couldn't get a word out. The cop didn't pick me up on that, though. He simply took it for granted. "Don't you know better than to leave a car with the wheels half-way out in the middle of the highway?"

"I'm sorry, Officer, I... I didn't think...." My voice did

not sound like me at all. It was high and quavering, like the voice of a very old man.

"Well, next time, think. That's how accidents happen. I'll let it go now, but watch it in the future. I know this is a lonesome stretch, but cars do come by here once in a while, and we get plenty of accidents."

He was telling me.

All at once he looked down at my clothing. His eyes narrowed. I wanted to look down there, too, but I didn't dare. I imagined—and then suddenly I was sure—I was covered with mud or blood, or maybe Haskell's name was written all over the vest, or maybe...

"Say," the cop said, "what were you doing down there, anyhow?"

I felt the corners of my mouth twitching to beat the band. At that minute I wanted to confess everything. The desire was so strong I had to fight myself. Because the suspense was pulling me to pieces, I don't think I ever wanted anything more. I was certain the cop suspected something queer and that it would only be a matter of seconds before he hiked down into the gully and had a look for himself. I opened my mouth to blurt it all out and take my chances with a jury. But then I shut it again and clamped my teeth together.

"Oh yeah, I see," the cop said. "Well, next time be sure your car is off the road."

I nodded without understanding.

"And you'd better button up, Johnny. You're wide open."

"Thanks, officer," I managed to say. "I will."

"I notice you're from the big town. I was wondering if by chance you know my brother? His name is Sid Hammerford."

"Sorry, I don't."

"Too bad. I figured it was pretty much of a long shot. He works for the Metropolitan Life Insurance Company there."

"No, I don't remember anyone by that—Say wait a

minute! Did he have red hair like yours, sort of a flat nose...?"

I thought I'd keep him in conversation and get his mind off the gully.

"Nope. Not Sid. He's short and darker than you."

"Well, then I guess it's a different guy."

"Yeah. Must be. Sid, he lives up in the Bronx, around Moshulu Parkway."

"No, I'm sure I don't know him."

"He's been in the east for almost eight years now. I hear from him every once in a blue moon. I was just hoping... well, thanks, anyway. And say, take it easy along in here. There's a washout about three miles ahead."

I stood in the road, watched him mount his cycle, kick the starter and then ride off. I was too dazed from fright to move. I began to sob hysterically, like a woman. Strange sounds came involuntarily from my throat, high and silly and weird. I tasted salt and knew I was crying. Then, all of a sudden, I sprang into the car, pressed the rumble-seat button, pulled out my half-filled valise, and flung it down into the gully. If they found a dead man now, it would be me. I fastened down the top on the right hand side of the car as I drove off. It was still raining, and the drops streaked down the windshield like tears.

II. SUE HARVEY

I was a fool to have let him—but it was done. Done, done, done, done....

That word kept drumming in my ears like a funeral march all the way home in the car. I was trying to coax myself to calm down, to forget it, and never to let such a thing happen again. But it didn't calm me and I couldn't forget it and I felt miserable and even worse than that.

I wanted to cry, and it was all I could do to hold myself in. Why give him the satisfaction of seeing me shed tears, I told myself, proving it had made a difference? He might begin to think I was in love with him, or perhaps that I was having a crying jag. Men can't understand women—at least regarding things like that.

When a man gets finished, he's through; his appetite's been satisfied, except that now he wants a plate of ham and eggs. We girls are quite another story. We have emotions and what not. We feel things. Any woman will know what I'm talking about. So I felt terrible.

Oh, I had made slips before—who hasn't?—but this one wasn't quite the same, because I'd known all along what he was planning to do and what to expect.

Good heavens, his manners were obvious enough, and the technique he employed had whiskers on it so long it would have fallen flat in the Middle Ages. Then, too, I hadn't been so drunk I wasn't able to see whatever there was to look at.

Yet, without being taken by surprise, and with every chance in the world to stop him, he got what he wanted. Oh, I struggled all right, told him I didn't like him that much, that I hardly knew him, that I was in love with someone else, and anyway, pu-lease, I was not that kind of a girl; I even slapped him once or twice, hard. But after saying "No!" about a dozen times, something happened, something that had never happened to me before. Although I still did not want him to have me, I found my "No!" getting just a trifle weaker; and then, curiously, all fight drained out of me and I gave up struggling entirely.

In the end, I didn't exactly give myself to him.

He took me.

Don't ask me why or how or when. I asked myself the same thing until my head spun. I didn't love the man—that much I was certain—nor did I even like him, when it came to that. He was very handsome and an actor and all the rest of it, but he was also the vainest, most self-centered individual I had ever run across.

When he finally won the argument about going to his apartment, did he show me etchings, a picture of his mother, or the customary rare something or other bachelors always have in their apartments? He did not.

He brought out his scrapbook. And after all the build-up he had been giving himself I was a little surprised to discover that although he had plenty of press notices, most of them were no larger than a postage stamp.

But I didn't hate him, even after it was all over. If I hated anyone, it was myself for having been so foolish. It made my cheeks burn when I realized what he must think of me: a little tramp, just another Hollywood pushover. What else could he think?

In my shame I almost wished I was in love with the man. Then I could ease my conscience by telling myself it had been foreordained—even if he didn't know it, the conceited thing.

I sat silently in the car, angry with myself and with him, at the same time trying to solve the problem of how it had happened.

I had never set eyes on him before seven o'clock when he drove in and ate dinner, tipping me a little too liberally. When he came back at eleven we began talking. Then, at twelve, when he asked to drive me home because it was raining, I began to suspect something. At first I refused, of course; but later, when I began to think of the long ride home on the bus, and how the buses were usually irregular at that hour, and how harmless he looked... Well, never again, I told myself.

While these reflections were further upsetting me he drove along the deserted streets whistling contentedly. Men are lucky that way. They can quickly forget things they prefer not to remember, and no matter what it is they have done, there are scarcely any distasteful after effects, recriminations or—worse yet—abortions. Then they wonder why a girl thinks it over a long time before she gives in! He pulled into the drive-in stand on Melrose where I worked and tooted the horn. Inside, I could see Mr. Bloomberg poke Selma into activity. She snatched up her trays, water, napkins and menu-cards and came running out through the drizzle. When she recognized the car she doubled her speed.

"Hello, Raoul," she said breathlessly. "Where're you been keeping yourself? We haven't seen you around here in a month." Then she glanced over and spied me. The smile on her face faded a little.

"Why, Sue! What are you doing up at this hour? I thought you said you were going straight home."

"Hello, Selma. I thought so, too." Selma shot a sharp look at Raoul, who pretended to be occupied with the menu. "I get it," she murmured. "You missed Gwen, you know."

"What do you mean, I missed her?"

"Oh, didn't you know she was fired?"

"Fired!" That came as a shock. Gwen had worked for Bloomberg longer than any of us.

"Well," explained Selma, "the boss found out today that she was married, and you know the rule. Gee, I hated to see her go-"

"I'll take coffee and a barbecued beef sandwich," announced Raoul. "Save the chatter until later."

"White, rye or wheat?"

"On a roll."

"And you?"

"I don't know."

"How about the same, Sue?"

"I'm not hungry."

I was beginning to wonder about Selma. Was Raoul one of her old boy friends? She was acting strangely. Although I didn't know Selma any too well, this much I did know: she didn't say much and she controlled her temper. One night when a drunk tried to kiss her she had acted much as she was acting now—friendly in her speech, but cold in her stare. Now, as she leaned against the door of the car waiting for our orders, there was something about her that made me think she was jealous.

"Oh, come now. You've got to eat something. The panic isn't on, you know."

"Really, Raoul, I'm not hungry in the least."

To tell the truth, I was feeling a little uneasy in my stomach. While the liquor I had put away was all good stuff, there had been too many kinds of it.

"Well, have some coffee. It'll sober you up."

That remark rubbed me the wrong way, but I let it go. When Selma brought the coffee I sipped it slowly, still thinking what an idiot I'd been ever to have allowed him to take me home—which he hadn't, as yet. The man was entirely without tact. The least he could have done was select another place to eat. Especially if Selma was one of his ex-girl friends. What was he trying to do? Give the help something to talk about? Parade his conquest of me before the late shift? Show them it had only taken him from midnight when I got of work, until... whatever time it was now?

"You might have picked another place to come," I told him.

He turned to look at me blankly, every inch the fake Englishman. "What's the matter with this? The food's good. At any rate, there aren't many places open at this hour, you know." He took out a package of imported cigarettes, tapped one of them on his thumb-nail and lighted it.

"There are plenty of places open along the Boulevard and on Vine," I retorted sharply. "We could have gone to the Coco Tree." It rankled me because he hadn't offered me a cigarette before lighting one himself. I didn't really want one, but who wouldn't be irritated to think that once somebody had you he was taking you for granted? Especially a person like Raoul Kildare, with his Hollywood-British accent and his installment plan Cadillac. A bit-player in the bargain. Ye gods, what was this town doing to me? With my looks I should have been working in the studios, not hopping cars in a Melrose Avenue hot-dog stand; going around with directors and producers and even stars, not with nobodies like Mr. Kildare. As jealous as girls usually are, even the ones I worked with agreed on that point. But what was there to do if the studios refused to test me? Two of them had promised they would, but, as I soon found out, in Hollywood promises don't count. The only person in town I could count on to get me in was Mr. Fleishmeyer, who was an agent, and fat, and old, but not too old. However, as anxious as I was to break in, I was not ready for Mr. Fleishmeyer.

Raoul had nothing more to say to me. When he finished eating he just sat there with the empty tray clamped to the door over his lap, running his fingers through his silky blond hair. He was only too well aware of the fact that he was handsome, so he affected this gesture of mussing himself up as though he didn't give a hang about his appearance. Nevertheless, I noticed that he was always careful not to ruin the part. Oh, I was on to him from the first and not one of his little tricks escaped me. The man was Hollywood personified; from the open-necked polo shirt and tweed sports jacket to the silk scarf knotted around his throat. There were thousands like him in town, each one trying terribly hard

to be different, each one a Greek god, walking around
and spilling glamour all over the streets for the benefit of
the tourists.

It seemed scarcely believable, but only a few months
before I too had thought Hollywood a glamorous place. I
had arrived so thoroughly read-up on the misinformation
of the fan magazines that it took me a full week before I
realized that the "Mecca" was no more than a jerkwater
suburb which publicity had sliced from Los Angeles—a
suburb peopled chiefly by out and out hicks (the kind of
dumbbells who think they are being wild and
sophisticated if they stay up all night) or by Minnesota
farmers and Brooklyn smart alecks who think they know
it all. I soon saw that there were only two classes of
society: the suckers, like myself, who had come to take
the town; and the slickers who had come to take the
suckers. Both groups were plotters and schemers and
both on the verge of starvation.

There was also a third group which I'd heard about
and read about but never seemed to come in contact
with: those who were actually under contract. From what
I understood, these fortunates barricade themselves in
their magnificent Beverly Hills or Bel-Air estates for fear
someone might want to borrow a dollar.

And Vine Street at Hollywood Boulevard, the so-
called Times Square of the West, reminded me of the
outside of an Eighth Avenue poolroom. There were more
well-dressed young men (who obviously were bums)
hanging around in front of the Owl Drug Store, the
barber shop and the Brown Derby than any place I had
ever been before. They made themselves obnoxious by
whistling at the girls and passing crude, audible
remarks. Also, they seemed to have X-ray eyes focused
on strangers' pockets to count their change. I honestly
believe that if somebody were foolish enough to drop a
quarter on the pavement, twenty or thirty Esquire
fashion plates would be trampled to death in the rush.

And where, I asked myself, were all the beautiful

women the fan magazines raved about? I had expected to
have very tough competition, but, frankly, most of the
girls were nothing extraordinary. The ones I passed on
the streets wore old slacks, cheap little sweaters and flat
heeled shoes. Either they had too much make-up on
their faces or none whatever. Nine-tenths of them ran
around with bandannas tied over their heads, like
immigrants stepping off Ellis Island, or as if they'd just
finished with the hairdresser. A person could almost read
Kansas, Iowa and Nebraska on their flat, countrified
faces.

All told, the town was a disappointment. There was
no glamour that I could see—unless twenty thousand or
so kids scrambling for a dollar is glamorous.

Then that wave came over me, that sudden suspicion
it was all a hoax, a frame-up plotted by the publicity-
greedy studios and the Chamber of Commerce to lure
people out here, away from their regular jobs, their
families and friends. The lies of the movie magazine's, the
lush literature of railroad companies and the exaggerated
salaries the press agents announced, all combined to
bait one of the foulest traps imaginable. And I was only
one of the little mice it had captured. It hadn't taken very
long. In less than six weeks time I was whipped and
broke, ready to work as a waitress and darned lucky to
get the chance. Oh, I still made the rounds, whenever
possible; but it was without much hope, and each time
with less confidence.

I sat there in the car, staring at the steady fall of
rain, at the flimsily constructed drive-in, at the dark
windows of a squat apartment house and at the
illuminated Paramount Pictures water-tower in the
distance. There was a heaviness in me which wasn't
caused by the drinks I'd put away, a pressure that
swelled up in my throat and threatened to burst. I was
sick of it all, thwarted. What was the use?

I tried to pull myself together. Lately these spells
were coming over me more and more often, making me

wish I was back in New York, working at the club and
living with Alex. I had been happy then—only I didn't
know it. Back east something like this never would have
happened. Alex would have been there. I turned to Raoul,
trying to keep my thoughts in the present. I didn't want
to think of New York; I didn't want to admit to myself
that I was homesick; and I couldn't bear to think of Alex,
especially so soon after I'd... "Come on. Please take me
home," I said to Raoul. "I've got an appointment
tomorrow afternoon at three."

"You mean today, don't you?"

"Today, then. What time is it, anyway?" He pulled up
his sleeve and made sure I noticed his elegant gold wrist-
watch.

"Five-ten."

"Let's go home," I moaned. "I'll never make it."

"All right. But first I want another cup of coffee."
When Raoul brought the car to a stop in front of the
bungalow he surprised me. He actually made a move to
get out and see me to the door!

"Never mind, Raoul," I said. "I can find my way in all
right by myself. It's raining and there's no sense you
getting drenched too. Good night."

I reached for the door-handle quickly, lest he try to
kiss me good night. I didn't feel like being kissed. The
mood I was in, I could cheerfully have murdered
someone—I didn't care who. I felt common and unclean.

Raoul caught me by the arm. "Wait a moment, Sue.
We haven't made any arrangements about seeing each
other again. I don't even know your phone number."

I hesitated. I didn't want to start any arguments at
that hour; I wasn't up to it. If I told him I never wished to
see him again, that tonight was all a mistake and I didn't
care pins for him, he would demand that I tell him why
not, what had he done to deserve this treatment and so
forth. On the other hand, if I gave him my phone number
and said good night as though everything was quite all
right and as it should be, the chances were he'd plague

me to death in the future. I didn't want that to happen. I'd had quite enough of Mr. Raoul Kildare.

While I was trying to decide which was the better course to pursue, he was taking out his address book and a fountain-pen. He seemed so cocksure of himself, so confident I would want to go out with him again, that my temper was aroused and I brought him up short. I wanted to hurt him, to puncture and deflate that enormous ego of his. Thank God, I thought, there is one weapon a woman can employ, more effective than biting or scratching or any other form of violence.

"I'm sorry, Raoul. I didn't like you," I said, swiftly. "I didn't like you and I don't particularly care to see you again, ever."

"What was that? What...?"

Then it began to dawn on him and he was so flabbergasted that the pen with which he was writing my name slipped out of his hand and rolled away in the dark. "Why... why, what do you mean, Sue? I'm afraid I don't quite get you."

"You get me, all right." He started to open his mouth to say something but evidently found nothing he could say. By his expression I saw that he was trying to persuade himself he had misunderstood the implication.

"You're not a good lover," I went on quietly, fully aware of the wound my words were inflicting.

"I don't have to make it any plainer, do I?"

There was a jubilance in me for the first time in ages. I watched him flinch and I knew I had struck home, into the most vulnerable spot in the man's armor. Most men, of course, think they are incomparable when it comes to making love; but Raoul even more so. The arrogant way he carried his head and the condescending air he had with me proved that only too conclusively. Honestly, I believe the man had actually considered he had done me a favor! Well, this would take some of the wind out of his sails for a long time. While I was conscious that it wasn't exactly ladylike for me to come out with bold statements of that nature, I couldn't resist the urge. In a way it helped to avenge poor Alex.

Raoul couldn't find his tongue. His mouth hung open and he stared blankly at me with perhaps the most astonished look on his handsome face I had ever seen. He appeared so forlorn that I felt a momentary touch of pity for him. What I had said, of course, was untrue, so absolutely false that I could scarcely believe he had swallowed it.

"Good night, Raoul," I said sweetly, perversely driving in the nail deeper. "At least I enjoyed looking at your scrapbook."

"Good night." He breathed the words so mournfully that I almost relented and kissed him good night. He was dazed, like a prizefighter who has just been dealt one below the belt. I stood outside the door of the bungalow fishing in my purse for the latch-key and watched the violet tail-lights of Raoul's Cadillac disappear down the winding, rain-swept street. I could hear the musical note of his horn when he sounded it at the Beachwood corner. It was a gay sound, so out-of-place in the gloom of early morning, reflecting nobody's feelings at that hour, especially not my own.

It was rotten of me, I decided, to have said that to him. Certainly it was the last word in cruelty. Why, something on that order, coming from a girl, was enough to ruin a man for life—to instill a complex, a fixation, or whatever the psycho-analysts chose to label it. Yes, the man did need taking down; but not to that extent. Probably that superior air of his was not his nature, but merely a defense. In Hollywood a person has to think highly of himself—because if he doesn't, who will? In any event it wasn't Raoul's fault I had been weak or crazy...

What on earth had possessed me to give myself to a stranger when I was in love with Alex? It hadn't been sheer need. My physical make-up doesn't require much attention. Oh, I'm not emotionally cold, by any means, but... well, good lord, not with anyone!

The heavy fog that usually accompanies the California dawns was gradually lifting and the rain for the moment had stopped. I could barely make out the Hollywood sign erected on the mountain at the far end of Beachwood canyon. I remembered the story of the number of girls who had committed suicide from that sign and the legend of the onetime silent-picture star who had climbed to the top of the letter "W" and thrown herself off. A dramatic death, stagy yet suitable. It was a source of wonder to me that there weren't many more suicides, what with so many people coming out, burning their bridges behind them—only to find disillusionment and failure.

My slight hangover was making me morbid. I shivered and unlocked the door. I'm usually not a brooding type, but five-thirty in the morning with rain and fog and a guilty conscience as props is not exactly a musical-comedy setting. Without switching on the lights, I tiptoed into the living-room.

The girl with whom I shared the bungalow worked days in the Columbia wardrobe department. She had to get up at seven each morning in order to punch in on time. For that reason she always crabbed about my late hours. She was a sweet kid and I'd known her for a long time, but when her sleep was interrupted she raised the roof. Without fail, almost every night when I arrived home she'd sit up in bed, all cold-creamed and kit-careered, and mutter: "Why don't you ask your boss to change your shift? For the love of Mike, here I am trying to catch a little sleep so I can get up at seven, and you... Now don't you dare cut off that alarm, Sue Harvey! You remember what I told you last time! I'm sorry it wakes you up when it goes off, but I've got a good job and I intend to keep it." Then she would roll over, pound the pillow viciously with her fist and be asleep again in less than two minutes. Poor Ewy. She had to put up with plenty.

We lived in a bungalow-court, our unit consisting of

a small living-room, a smaller bedroom, a tiny kitchen and a bath so infinitesimal that the sink overhung the tub. Ewy claimed you could brush your teeth at the same time you took a bath. Perhaps you could; I never tried it. The place was furnished with the customary cheap brand of over-stuffed furniture, faded carpets and the odds and ends of about five different sets of dishes. The rent was thirty-two dollars a month, with gas and lights extra—which wouldn't have been bad when it was divided by two. Unfortunately, very often Ewy would succumb to her weakness for gambling and lose her entire week's wages in a phone room during lunch-hour. She could pick them, but usually wrong. Like the Hollywood population in general, we were always behind with the landlord. But the place itself, while neat and inexpensive, had, like every other apartment in Hollywood, an air of impermanency. You felt that if you stood in the center of the living-room and shouted: "Strike it, boys!" the whole place would fold up and disappear like a set in a very few seconds.

It was small wonder there were so many cases of homesickness in town.

My customary way of entering was to slip off my shoes and try to creep into the bathroom to undress. Once or twice I had successfully accomplished this, but this time I heard Ewy sit up in bed and fumble for the light cord. Since there was no longer any point in trying to be stealthy, I stomped into the bedroom.

"Did I wake you, Ewy? I tried to be as quiet as I could. "

Ewy found the little string and the lights went on. Still half-asleep, she felt around on the floor by her bed until she found the alarm clock. It was twenty minutes to six. She gave me a look which said: a-fine-time-to-be-coming-in and flopped back on to her pillow with a martyr's sigh.

"I'm sorry, Ewy. I couldn't help it. I was on a party. Why don't you stuff cotton in your ears at night like I suggested?"

"And how would I hear the alarm when it goes off?" She grumbled and pounded her pillow. "Call the Fleishmeyer Agency tomorrow morning before noon. He's been wearing out the phone all evening. God, that man's persistent. "

"You didn't tell him what I was doing, did you?"

"Naturally not."

"Fine. It wouldn't do me much good having people know I'm hopping cars. Someday I might need Manny Fleishmeyer."

"Well, if you play around with him, you ought to have your head examined. He reminds me of a toad, and not a handsome toad at that. And yes, I almost forgot. There's a letter for you. Came in the afternoon mail. I stuck it in the bathroom on top of your cold-cream jar—or my cold-cream jar, to be exact, if you'll pardon the implication—so you'd be sure to find it."

"Alex?"

"How should I know? I didn't open it."

I began to pray it would be from Alex. He hadn't written for such a long time—months and it worried me. I was so used to hearing from him regularly once a week. Of course it was my own fault. I hadn't kept up my end of the correspondence because there really was nothing to write about. I didn't have the cheek to write lies to him like I did to mother, saying that I was doing splendidly, that the studios would soon be fighting for me, etc. Alex would know better.

As I hurried into the bathroom and felt around in the dark for the envelope, I had his name on my lips. I needed Alex that night more than I had ever needed him before. Just his familiar scrawl would help me to get out of the rotten mood I was in, would surely aid in forgetting the impossible thing I'd done. Alex was a dear. He was a clumsy old thing, bashful as a schoolboy, and, except for his music, a dummy; but I adored him. Although he was occasionally annoying, he alone had the power to quiet my nerves whenever they might be on edge. Sometimes his solicitousness would make things worse, but soon I couldn't help but love him for his clumsy attempts to please me. It was practically impossible to stay angry with him for any length of time. If I spoke harshly to him I was always instantly sorry, for he hurt easily.

Reviewing our affair, I decided it must have been one of those everyday cases of love at first sight. I had first taken notice of him during a chorus rehearsal when he stood up and asked Bellman's permission to leave the room. He wasn't trying to be funny, either. He really had to go. Of course everyone laughed and he blushed like a child. Then, when one of the girls offered him her hat, he got so flustered and looked so pathetic up there on the stand, that it went to my heart. I felt like running up and kissing him, the boob. Yes, he was a boob. I had to work on him all of three weeks before the poor fish even asked to take me out. I threw myself in his path at every opportunity and flashed him my prettiest smiles; I asked him the time and would he give me a cigarette and match. Finally, after a siege, when I kissed him good night for the first time, he didn't even make a move to follow it up. Perhaps he was frightened or bashful or something, I don't know. Men are funny, sometimes. A girl can semaphore every signal in the book before the fellow wakes up and finds the war is over. Now Raoul....

The letter was not from Alex. When I carried it into the bedroom I saw it was from my mother, with the usual sob story and broad hint. She could use this; she could use that. Mother could always use something, the old parasite. If only she knew how tough it was for me to lay my hands on a few dollars! I don't suppose it is very nice for a daughter to talk about her mother that way but what had she ever done for me? Bear me, that's all. And probably she would have avoided that if she hadn't been such a rabid Catholic. Just the way she talked to Alex that day when he tried to reinstate me alone was enough to sour me on her for life. We had done nothing wrong.

We were having an affair, yes. But we loved each other and Alex would have married me in a minute if I'd said the word. Anyway, what right had she to complain? She wasn't the one who had to worry...

Which reminded me.

I couldn't afford to waste another minute.

Glancing through the letter to satisfy my curiosity, I discovered that it was some lighter clothes this time. New York was hot and she was running around in a fall suit. I ripped the letter up and flung the pieces into the trash-basket by the writing-desk. The next day was pay-day. I'd send her five dollars. Oh, I knew it was foolish. The chances were she'd drop half of it into the collection-plate.

"For the love of Pete," Ewy groaned, "turnout the light and get into bed! Or go into the living-room."

"All right. Good night, Ewy."

"Good night hell! Good morning!"

I scooped up a nightie and went into the bathroom, locking the door after me. I had things to do and it would be a good half-hour before I was ready to hit the pillow. I undressed rapidly, at the same time looking at my face in the medicine chest mirror. My eyes were a little bloodshot from staying up so late, but still lovely. I had been told many times that my eyes are the nicest part of my anatomy—tie score with my breasts—because they are an unusual shade of green; not a jade green, a much darker color. I pressed my face as close as I could get it to the glass and examined them. There were tears glistening in them now as I thought of Alex. The gleam was an improvement because it covered up the redness. Where was Alex? Had he moved from the old apartment?

He must have; because unless he was working again , how could he pay the rent? That was probably why he had never answered the post card I sent him.

"I love you, Alex," I whispered into the mirror—playing a little scene. "I'll always love you."

It was a trifle overdone. In movie parlance, I was

mugging it. I felt the emotion all right, only reality on the
screen always photographs funny. To be any good you
have to underplay everything. A casting director told me
that. I tried it again, this time changing the inflection,
expressing as much as I could just with my eyes and
keeping my voice as flat as possible. "I love you, Alex. I'll
always love you. And no matter what happens, I'll always
be waiting." Once more. God, I felt it surge all through
me. At that moment I loved Alex more than ever. I did, I
did. It was intense. It pulled at me and brought more
tears into my eyes. Soon they were rolling down my
cheeks. "I'll always love you. And no matter what
happens, I'll always be waiting...."

It was great, a natural. Who said I couldn't act? Of
course it wasn't all acting. I repeated the scene two or
three times more, experimenting with tone, quality and
diction. Then I ran hot water and looked around for the
douche.

III. ALEXANDER ROTH

Start your sermon. I'll listen to it. But I know what you're going to hand me even before you open your mouths. You're going to tell me that I'm nothing but a common tramp, a thief and a no-good grave-robber. You're going to say you don't believe my story of how Haskell met his death, and give me that don't-make-me laugh expression on your smug faces. You're going to say, "Roth, for God's sake, why not make a clean breast of it? You're not kidding anyone." You're going to harp on that old gag about confession being good for the soul.

Or maybe you're going to break open the hymnal and tell me I should have waited for the police and had faith in the Lord? I'm not sacrilegious, but even if the Lord is my shield and my buckler, who the hell is going to be my attorney?

So if you can, just put yourself in my position before you let off steam and warn me for my own good that isn't the way to get to heaven. I wasn't trying to get to heaven. All I was trying to do was to get to Los Angeles, to see Sue, and, if possible, to ace myself into pictures. Now what I had aced myself into was a murder—or what looked like one—and I was the murderer in every respect, except that I didn't kill the guy. I had his car and his dough and his clothes, all right; but that was all. I didn't have his life. Maybe I'd never find out, but Haskell could have died of heart failure, of liver trouble, of cancer, of any of a million things. If that crack on the head was what killed him, I wasn't to blame. Nevertheless, as I drove away from the spot I kept telling myself over and over that I should have taken the northern route or stayed put in New York. I wish I had. Take it from me, it was a mighty queer feeling pulling into a service station and telling the fellow to fill her up. I'd only owned one car before in my life, and you can bet it wasn't a big beauty like the one I was driving. What I had in New York was a heap, if there ever was one. A still more uncomfortable feeling though, than driving around in a car that wasn't mine, was whipping out Haskell's roll and paying for the gas. I couldn't get accustomed to the idea that now the dough was mine, and I kept mental count of every penny I spent as if Haskell would show up any minute and ask for his change.

"Check your oil, sir?"

Check my oil. That was a hot one.

"No, that's all right. I changed it a while back. "

I was afraid to stop too long. Maybe someone already had found the body and the cops were on my tail. I was hot and, boy, did I know it. I wouldn't feel safe until after I ditched the car.

"Here you are, sir. Thank you. Call again."

"Sure, sure."

I grabbed the change the attendant held out and stuffed it into my pocket. Without waiting to count it, I let in the clutch with a jerk that shot the Buick out into the middle of the road.

Distance, brother. That's what I wanted to put between me and the place on Route 70. I'll never be able to wipe off the slate. Even as I drove along I could see it before my eyes; ahead was a slight bend in the road to the left, with a white guard-railing and a SLOW sign; to the right, on the far side of the gully, was a tree, the only decent-sized tree around, only a few inches shorter than the telephone pole alongside it; behind was a dip in the highway where a shallow puddle had formed. Yes, every last detail of the road, the ruts in the shoulder and the formation of the brush was clear. If I had been an artist I could have painted that scene accurately with out going back. But more than just that, I could see what was hidden beneath the growth of brush down in the gully. I could see a twisted form in blue pants and a maroon polo-shirt with a ripped collar.

I gave the Buick everything. I rolled it up to eight-five, to ninety on the straight parts. On the curves the rear wheels skidded and screamed and this made me look in the mirror. I kept imagining I was being followed and that I could faintly hear sirens way back in the distance.

Of course I knew it was dangerous, speeding like that. I was more apt to tangle with the law that way than by simply riding along at a reasonable rate. But I couldn't help myself. In Arizona the cops don't care how fast you travel through the desert—you drive at your own risk. However, in the townships they really clamp the lid on. I did slow down going through them, but my foot was itching to stamp on the accelerator.

More dangerous than cops were my eyes. Fear kept them wide open, in spite of which I felt myself dropping off to sleep. I'd suddenly realize that things were getting a little out of focus and that the road was fading gradually away. I had to struggle to stay awake. All this at eighty and eighty-five miles an hour over wet pavement.

Just how long it took me to cover the sixty-odd miles to the California State Line, I don't know. It must have been under an hour, but I'd lost all track of time. The rain had stopped and the sun was feebly trying to come out from behind some clouds when I drew up to the inspection booth at Ehrenberg. The two motor-cycle cops who were chewing the fat with the inspectors didn't make me feel any too happy, you can imagine. I put the car in second, resolving if they made any suspicious moves I'd make a run for it.

One of the cops walked over to the car, slowly, which was a good sign. "May I see your registration certificate and driver's license, please?"

All my life, ever since as a kid a cop cuffed me for playing football on the grass in Central Park, I have been a little leery of brass buttons. I've learned it is healthier to give the police a wide berth, because once they've got you pegged and you're in the Bastille you're completely at their mercy. Cops, as a rule, are overbearing and brutal, swollen up with their own authority which they abuse. Instead of being public servants, they bully the public and treat ordinary citizens like criminals. In spite of the law to the contrary, in a station-house a man is guilty unless he can prove an alibi. Now, after my experiences with the law in Dallas, this gentlemanly treatment came as a surprise, until I remembered that I was sitting in an expensive automobile. Cops know dough and influence go hand in hand. For all this fellow knew, I was a friend of some big shot official who controlled the strings which transferred little shots on and off these gravy jobs.

I dug into the wallet and found the papers. The cop glanced at me and then at the description on the license, checked the registration with the plates, and handed them back with a nod. I took the car out of gear.

"Carrying any fruits or vegetables?"

"No."

"Any livestock, poultry?"

I thought I'd play it funny and then maybe nobody would notice I was nervous and shaking to beat the band. "I don't think so, officer," I said. "But if you should happen to find a couple of Maryland chickens back there, let me know."

The copper smiled and went back to help one of the inspectors who was fooling around, trying to open the rumble. I pressed the button for him. He stuck his head in and pulled out a carton of canned goods, a blanket and a big alligator-skin traveling bag. He poked around for a minute in the carton and put it back where he had found it. The bag he took over to the booth to inspect.

Then I remembered and went cold. My heart began to pound like a trip-hammer. Suppose there was more of that marihuana in the bag? That would be poetic justice, wouldn't it? Me being nailed on a Federal narcotic ticket for what he had been carrying... But I guess Haskell wasn't that dumb. If there was any more stuff in the car, it wasn't in the bag. The inspector re-packed it, snapped it shut and tossed it back into the rumble. I knelt on the seat and banged it before he changed his mind and decided to take another look.

"Just visiting California, Mr. Haskell?"

"Yes, just visiting."

God, it was funny being called Haskell.

"Well, remember, if you're employed and stay more than thirty days you have to get California plates."

"All right, officer. But I'll only be in California a short time."

"How are things back in New York, anyway? I haven't seen the place in over ten years."

"Oh, the same as always. They've got a few more buildings up, that's all."

"Well, I'd sure like to take a trip back, one of these days. I've got a brother there now. He's in the liquor business."

"Is that so?" It seemed as though everybody had relatives in New York. New York was made up of brothers and sisters and cousins of people in Arizona and California.

"It's O.K. You can go ahead now."

They slapped a sticker on the windshield and waved me on. I damned near stalled the car for the second time on account of my shaky knees which, for the life of me, I couldn't get under control. My heart didn't stop thumping until I'd covered the two and a half miles into Blythe.

I couldn't drive any farther without some sleep. I was completely pooped. Cops or no cops, I knew I had to hit the hay and hit it hard, even if they got me for it. I would have preferred driving on through as far as Mecca and sleeping there, because Blythe was too close to the Arizona border for comfort; but that would mean another ninety or a hundred miles, so I said to myself, nothing doing.

There was an auto-court on the left, half a block off the main stem, and I pulled into it. It was just a group of ten or twelve shacks with places to park cars alongside, but it spelled home sweet home in big letters. Actually, what it spelled was: The Morning Glory Tourist Rest—Day or Weekly Rates.

When I sounded the horn, a girl came running out of the shack marked OFFICE and hopped on the running-board. Even in my overwrought condition I couldn't help noticing that she wasn't bad at all; a little thin in the face, maybe, but her eyes were clear and she had nice shafts and a cute round keister. Of course, put her next to Sue and she'd look like thirty cents—but then most women would. "Hello," she smiled. "Are you looking for a cabin?"

"That's right, baby."

"Well, you've come to the right place Are you alone, sir?"

Tired as I was, I thought I'd kid with her a little. It's weakness of mine that when I see some pretty rural talent I play for the laughs.

"No, I'm not alone, sister," I replied with a dead pan. "Can't you see my grandmother's ghost sitting right here beside me?"

She laughed, proving that her teeth were white and even, with no cavities. "Well, we won't charge you for your grandmother. If you'll drive straight back, I'll show you and the old lady a cabin."

"Not too near the music."

I crept down the line of bungalows until she signaled me to stop in front of one of them. I cut the switch, opened the rumble, pulled out Haskell's bag and followed her inside. It was the usual auto-camp shack, except that this one had a bathroom.

"See? Bath, shower, towels, soap. And a nice roomy double bed."

"Not so roomy. Grandma tips the scales at two-fifty."

"Oh, my!" She gave it one of those shocked, Zasu

Pitts readings that evidently she thought was kind of clever. Then she dropped into a chair.

As soon as she did that, I had a hunch if I wanted her I could have her along with the cabin at no additional cost. People usually don't sit down when they're renting cabins, unless they're tired or want to get acquainted. This dame wasn't tired. But I didn't want her. Man, I was so worn out from worrying and driving that if the most beautiful woman in the world had climbed into my bed, I would have shoved her out and gone back to sleep. And this little number, not bad really, was certainly not the most beautiful woman in the world. Then, too, there was Sue to think about.

The two times I had been unfaithful to her were months ago. With luck I'd see her in a day or two and I didn't want this on my conscience.

"All right. No bed bugs, eh?"

She looked hurt.

"Then it'll do. How much?"

"Only three."

"Come again?"

She was a little peeved that I wasn't following her lead on the chair angle. It showed all over her face. Her voice got flat.

"I said three dollars for the night."

I shook my head. "You've got me wrong, sister. I don't want to buy the place."

I turned to walk out. I know how those places are run. They charge you according to the car you're driving. If I had pulled in with an old wreck, probably she wouldn't have asked more than a deuce. Mileage isn't the only disadvantage in owning a big bus. However, I really had no intention of leaving The Morning Glory Tourist Rest. I decided if she didn't call me back before I reached the car, I'd pay her price, even if it was a fin. I was so tired, I doubt if I would have been able to turn the ignition switch.

"All right, then. Two and a half."

"It's a deal."

I put the suit-case back on the bed, peeled off two
singles, fished out four-bits and she left without a word. I
felt rather ashamed of myself then. She had only tried to
be nice and I had treated her rotten. It might have been a
different story if I hadn't been so dead....

But I was. And don't let any more of these novel-
writers tell you that when a man is in trouble or has
something on his mind he has nightmares or can't sleep
and goes haywire and runs to the cops to confess. That's
bunk. I slept like a top for almost eighteen hours and, as
far as I know, I was too busy sleeping to dream about a
thing.

When I awoke it was three the following morning. I
had been too groggy the night before to unpack Haskell's
grip, so I had piled into bed wearing my shorts. The first
thing I did was rip them off and hop into the shower. The
Morning Glory must have been run properly because
even at that hour the water was hot and I enjoyed a good
scrub. When I came out, massaging myself with a thick
towel, I felt like a new man. I had been so dirty before,
that cleaning up seemed to change the whole complexion
of things—which, of course, it did. I was glad and even a
little surprised to see that I was a white man.

Whistling, I went back into the other room and
opened Haskell's suit-case. There were two
compartments in it: one contained some shirts, socks,
underwear, toilet articles and a mess of papers—letters
and things; while the other side held two suits of clothes,
a pair of shoes, some ties, handkerchiefs, a bathrobe and
a pair of slippers. I made a dive for his razor and, ten
minutes later, I had left six days' growth of beard all over
the sink. Haskell had some kind of after-shave lotion
there, too. I slapped some of it on me. It stung for a
minute but then it felt great.

Next came the problem of what to put on—or was it a
problem? I took a pair of his silk shorts, a clean pair of
socks, one of his shirts with the initials "C.J.H."

embroidered on the pocket, the least annoying of his ties and dressed myself in a different suit. It was a single-breasted blue herring-bone tweed, a honey of a tailoring job with patch-pockets in the coat and high-waisted trousers. The stuff I had on the day before was still in good shape, of course, but well... you know how you feel about wearing things a man's been dead in. I rolled up what I had been wearing and took it out to the car. Coming back in again, I caught a glimpse of myself in the bureau mirror and did a perfect double-take. I was a stranger to myself.

I was hungry as an unemployed actor. Remember, the last thing I put in my stomach was the steak Haskell bought me in Lordsburg. And don't forget where I lost it. However, I didn't want to leave the cabin before I had a look through his stuff. If I was going to be Mr. Haskell for a little while—at least until I crossed the desert—I'd better try to find out something about myself. That minute at the state line really scared me, to say nothing about the conversation with Trooper Hammersford. So I turned the suit-case upside down and began to go through every article systematically. I didn't miss a trick.

I didn't find out much from the wearing apparel. Whatever had a label in it had a New York label. His shirts and shorts were Lord and Taylor, his ties and pyjamas Finchley or Sulka, and the shoes he had packed were Florsheim. The bathrobe, a big woolly thing, had a J. Abercrombie label. I went through the pockets of everything and drew a blank. But the papers were a revelation. After reading through them, I began to see Mr. Haskell as I had never seen him before. It was evident from the stuff he was carting around in his own bag that he was not the open-handed, easy-going big-shot who threw away a dollar now and then and went around buying steak dinners for strange bums. Before I got done I saw him more as a chiseler and four-flusher. I could just picture the guy standing by his book at Empire, glad-handing the money and brushing off the down-andouters. You've seen that kind by the hundreds, hanging around your club or your place of business.

One letter in particular told me all I needed to know. It was a letter addressed to Mr. Charles J. Haskell, Sr., Bellagio Road, Bel-Air Estates, Westwood, California. I guessed that this must be his father and Haskell had forgotten to mail it. But before I tore it open, I turned my attention to the wallet.

There were seven hundred and sixty-eight dollars in that billfold, in fifties, twenties, and tens! Imagine, almost eight Cs! It took me all of twenty minutes to catch my breath and get used to the idea I was rich. I sat there on the bed and counted the dough over and over to make sure I hadn't counted the same bills twice.

In a compartment of the wallet I also found a cancelled bank book. The account was in the name of Charles Hanson and showed entries of six, seven and eight hundred dollars in July, swelling the total to a neat sum of fourteen thousand eight hundred dollars and a few cents interest. Then, on the seventh of August, there was a withdrawal of thirteen thousand five hundred dollars, and on the twelfth the balance was withdrawn and the account closed. Jesus, I thought, what high finance. It looked like the war debt to me. Well, anyway I had seven hundred and sixty-eight bucks of it. It was chicken-feed alongside of those figures; nevertheless, to Alexander Roth it was a fortune. Besides; those others were only figures and they won't pay your fare on a tram-car.

In the opposite compartment of the wallet was another little book, like an address book. I leafed through it. He had four or five addresses and phone numbers written down in there, most of them women, but I caught on at once that this was his pound-of-flesh list. He had Louie—$39, O'Hanlan—$158, Mr. Pepperman—$40, A. H. Burnside—$90; stuff like that marked dawn. It ran into about thirty pages, with here and there a line drawn through a name, signifying that whoever had owed the money had paid off. Just for the hell of it, I added up all the sums. The total was a little over ninety-six hundred smackers. There was one page in there labeled: P.D. WITH N.G. CHECKS. Nineteen names and addresses were listed under that and not one of them, curiously, was anybody I knew. In the back of the book he had some other junk written down which I couldn't make out—mostly figures. I guess maybe he'd been trying to figure odds or something. But at the bottom of the list, marked off from the rest of the page, was what looked to me like a diet; no alcohol, fruit juices, plenty of water, salvarsan.... I got it.

There wasn't much else in that wallet except a receipted bill from the Hotel Pennsylvania in New York, the car registration and his driver's licence. From the last mentioned I learned that I was now Charles J. Haskell, Jr., born September 7, 1905, having brown hair, brown eyes, being of the white race, six feet tall and weighing 170. What I was searching for were his trunk checks, but he didn't have any. I figured if he expressed his trunks and never picked them up there might be an investigation. I wouldn't care for any of that.

On the bed, among the rest of the papers, was a thick stack of I O U's—a good fifty of them, bound together with a rubber band. I tore those up and flushed them down the toilet. They were no good to me, no good to Haskell, and certainly no good to the people who'd written them.

That was one time a sucker got a break.

I found one letter there, addressed to Haskell at the Pennsylvania, that got my goat and created the impression that the guy who had bought me a steak wasn't such a prince among men at that. It was a short note from some fellow named Luther Walsh, begging Haskell (or Hansen, as he called him) to quit mailing post

cards to the office, reminding him he owed money for
bets. Walsh went on to say that at the moment his wife
was sick and he couldn't spare the dough to pay off., but
that he would mail Haskell the money just as soon as he
could. He said that if those post cards continued to come
to the office, the boss might see one of them; if he did, it
was good-bye job. The fella worked for a trust company of
same kind and the employees were not encouraged to
play the ponies. I looked Walsh up in Haskell's book. He
owed $25.

But it was the other letter, the one addressed to his
father, that interested me. It almost made me sick to
read it. Doesn't it get you sometimes in the solar plexus
to think how low a guy can sink? Once I had thought
Haskell was tops, but that letter reversed things. Before I
was half-way through that masterpiece of insincerity, I
think if the skunk had been standing in the room I'd
have let him have it! I told myself that old Charles, Sr.,
was pretty damned lucky his son disappeared, even if he
didn't know it. What was so bad about the letter? Oh, not
much. But wait, I'll give it to you in full. In case you feel
like I felt, the bathroom's to the left.

Dear Father,
I know you will be surprised to hear from me after all
this lapse of time, but I feel I can't stay away any longer. I
would like to come home for a while, if you'll have me,
and see you and Dolores again. No doubt you will think it
very strange that at this late date, I have grown
homesick, but the truth of the matter is / *always have
been.*

My reason in not having written before is that I was
conscious I was unworthy to be called your son and that
I'd done a shameful thing, the chances were you could
never forgive. Then too, I've been very busy traveling
around. You see, I am in business for myself, selling

prayer—and hymn-books to churches and Sunday-schools. As an ardent churchman that should be of interest to you. I remember how we used to attend services there on Sunset Boulevard every Sunday morning. I was only a boy then, of course, and I suppose I didn't fully appreciate the value of worship.

I do hope you will realize how changed I am; also that you have by this time managed to excuse the awful things I did fifteen years ago which caused me to run away. I must have been a very wild and willful brat.

Naturally, putting out Edward's eye was an accident—we were only playing with the swords—but when it happened it frightened me and I did the first thing that popped into my head.

Not only that, there was another reason for my disappearing which you doubtless know about. I was pretty sure you'd found out I stole Mother's engagement and wedding rings and pawned them. I never would have done it had I realized they were all you had left to remember her by. It was not for several years that the full significance of what I'd done began to dawn on me. Then, you can understand, I felt I could never come back.

Please, Father, let bygones be bygones.

When all this happened I was only sixteen or seventeen. Well, that must be all for now. I leave it in your hands. If the door will be open to me, you can expect me within a very few weeks. I will wire you a day or two before I arrive. Please convey my love to Dolores, who must be quite the lady these days.

I'm sorry I can't be more definite about the date of my arrival, for I have several churches I must visit on my trip across the country—and you know how ministers are. Until I see you then,

CHUCK.

A killer, eh? He hadn't caused his old man enough

worry and trouble as a kid; he intended to go back and finish the job. And with a plan as plain as the nose on our face. He'd get the old gent to stake him to thirty or forty grand for his hymn-book business, then chase off to Miami and sink it into a different kind of book. The old boy might raise particular hell when he caught wise, but what of it? He certainly wouldn't stick his own son in jail. Haskell knew that and was playing it for all it was worth. Why, it was duck soup in any language. Papa would be so tickled to see his little Chuck again that he'd part with the coin easily, especially since it was going to be invested in such a respectable enterprise, prayer-books and hymnals. I told you it would make you sick. Well, I guess God or Fate, or whatever that Something is, stepped in just at the nick of time and saved Charles J. Haskell, Sr., from taking a flyer in sacred literature preferred.

Now don't try to tell me that man is master of his own destiny. What happened to Haskell proves that you never can tell what's in the cards for you, and the road you aim to take nine times out of ten turns out to be a blind alley; either that, or it leads someplace quite different. If you think I'm all wet in this theory, you'll have to show me where.

Nevertheless, the letter made me feel somewhat easier in my mind. If it had been mailed, his family would be expecting him. When he never showed up they might grow worried and demand a police investigation. Working through the deserted car, the cops might trace me, and deliver Alexander Roth to the anxious family with the compliments of the Bureau of Missing Persons. No, thanks. It was lucky for me Haskell had neglected to mail the letter.

But wait a minute. Maybe he had mailed another letter. That was always possible. Maybe he had written one in which he was now a full-fledged Baptist minister, for all I knew. However, there was no use wondering if he had or not; I'd never find out, so to hell with it.

The rest of the papers were just a lot of junk and I was about to destroy them all—the letters, too—when something slipped out of the pile and fluttered to the floor. I picked it up and saw that it was a newspaper clipping of some kind, all about a hospital in Cleveland that had discovered a new way to sterilize instruments before an operation. For a second or two I couldn't understand why Haskell had cut it out; but then I had an idea and I turned it over.

That was the first and only time I actually felt guilty about what had happened. Up until that moment, Haskell was just a stranger, some guy I didn't know; but when I turned that clipping over I was introduced to his family.

It was nothing but a picture, pretty clear and sharp for a newspaper reproduction, but still a flat piece of paper with a lot of lines and shadows. Yet, it did something to me. I looked at it and something went snap inside of me, like an E string that's been tightened too much. It was a close-up of an old man and a rather pretty girl—very ordinary-looking people, really—dressed in light summer clothes. It was their eyes though that got me. They seemed to stare out of the picture into mine—and beyond, into whatever's back there. CHARLES J. HASKELL, WELL KNOWN WILMINGTON EXPORTER AND SPORTS FAN WITH HIS DAUGHTER AT THE BEVERLY HILLS TENNIS TOURNAMENT, the caption read. Not to me it didn't. What I saw there was a silent indictment and a chill ran up me. I crumbled the picture into a little ball and flushed it down the johnny. The rest of the papers, race programs and letters, followed suit.

When that was done, I re-packed the suitcase and straightened up the cabin. I cleaned off the sink, aired the bed, spread out the shower-curtain so it could dry, hung up the dirty towels where they belonged and then decided it was time to blow. I carried the bag out to the car, locked it in the rumble-seat and went on foot to find a place to eat. By this time it was five o'clock and there was only one place open in town, even though it was broad daylight. I headed for it and went in. It was one of those all-night dining car joints, greasy by tradition, yet with a nice smell to it. I grabbed a stool.

"Bacon and eggs, some cereal first, fried potatoes, toast with marmalade and a cup of coffee. Let me have the coffee now."

"Coming up."

While I sipped the steaming brown water they called coffee, I tried to forget Haskell and his family by concentrating on something pleasant: Sue. I had her address, of course. She was living on Cheremoya Avenue, near Beachwood Drive, wherever that might be. I could scarcely wait to see her shocked but pleased expression when she opened the door and recognized me. The chances were she'd all but faint; me being there in Hollywood and she thinking me three thousand miles away. I started to rehearse what I was going to say. "Good morning, madam. I represent the Marital Insurance Company. Please don't slam the door. I know you'll be interested in the policy I have to offer today. It safeguards the wife against the returning husband. What? You have no husband? Dear, dear. That's something I hadn't considered. In that case, madam, will you marry me?" No, not so hot. Maybe: "Good morning, madam. Is this Donnerwetter's Sanitarium? I'm Herr Professor-Doctor Heinrich von Lousenhitler. I have a patient, a Mrs. Noman de Lez, who has heard about this new Hollywood treatment." Worse yet. That stank on ice. "Quick, moll! Let me in and get the tommy from where I hid it in the baby's crib. I'm hot and the bulls got the place surrounded! Oh, oh. Too late. They got me!" That was lousy too—even if it was appropriate.

I'd made up my mind not to tell Sue about what happened. It wasn't that I mistrusted her, but why worry her after it was all over? And it would be over before I showed my face around her, I told myself. The last thing in the world I wanted was to jeopardize her. I'd make damned sure my hands were clean before I went hunting Cheremoya.

Probably I'd still be sitting there day-dreaming about Sue if the guy behind the counter hadn't shoved a bowl of oatmeal at me. "Did you want bacon and eggs or ham and eggs, buddy? I forgot."

I looked up at him and then I lost my appetite. I jerked suddenly and Haskell's sun-glasses fell from the counter and smashed. Two stools away sat a California State Trooper, drinking a glass of tomato juice.

"I've changed my mind."

"You changed your mind?" The fellow was dumb, all right. He couldn't understand the King's English.

"Yeah," I said, getting to my feet. "I'm not hungry any more. Cancel the order."

"What's the beef? Something wrong with the oatmeal?"

"No. Just not hungry."

"A fly somewhere, maybe?"

In answer, I threw a quarter on the counter and left in a walk. But once outside, I flew. I crossed the road, doubled back farther on down the street and then headed for the Morning Glory. Five minutes later I was miles away pushing the Buick along the road toward Mecca with the accelerator down to the floor-boards.

I don't know just when it struck me that I never was going to abandon that car, but it gradually dawned in my thick skull that, whether I liked or not, I would have to hold on to it. If I wanted to dispose of it, it was necessary that I do so through a legitimate sales transaction. A deserted automobile always leads to police inquiries regarding the whereabouts of its owner, and, naturally, any fool can see that to check up on Haskell was to check up on me. It was a pretty big risk, but what else was there for me to do but to keep on being Haskell until the ownership of the Buick was in someone else's name? Then, and no sooner, could I do what I liked.

There you'll go again, I suppose. You'll be telling me

that I'm a cock-eyed liar and the only reason I wanted to hang on to the car was because it was worth an easy eight hundred. Well, you're all wet on that score. My life is worth more to me than any eight hundred bucks; and if you think peddling that car wouldn't be dangerous, you're the one who's a dummy. Why, that car was so hot, whoever drove it would have to wear asbestos drawers.

I was beginning to suspect by that time it wasn't as simple as I'd imagined it was going to be when I left the dead man lying in the gully. I thought all there was to do was to get out of the vicinity, forget where I parked the car and continue on my merry way. Now I saw how carelessly I'd figured. Dressed in my clothes and with my valise, the police were sure to identify the corpse as one Alexander Roth, a vagrant on the Dallas blotter. Judge Lascoff's letter of reference in the valise would establish that much at once. I remembered gratefully that the judge had very poor eyesight. That would come in handy if he should be called upon by the coroner to inspect the remains. However, if a deserted car was found registered in the name of Charles Haskell and discovered to have passed through the Arizona and California state lines during the time it was possible the crime was committed, it is only logical to suppose that the cops might get the idea the body they found in the ditch was not the bum's body, Roth, but the body of the guy who owned the car. Linking the two wouldn't take much brilliance. If they should ever check into this theory and find it true, they'd know who they had to look for, all right. I could just see those Post Office placards: WANTED FOR QUESTIONING IN REGARD TO THE MURDER OF CHARLES HASKELL IN ARIZONA, ALEXANDER ROTH. AGE: 29, HEIGHT: 6 FT., WEIGHT: 170, BROWN HAIR AND EYES, SLIGHT BUMP AT BRIDGE OF NOSE, IS BELIEVED TO BE MUSICIAN BY PROFESSION, NO KNOWN ALIASES, LAST SEEN AT EHRENBERG, ARIZONA....

You see, I had to watch my step.

I reasoned I was comparatively safe so long as I

continued to play the part of Haskell and didn't bump into any members of his family. I would sell the car as soon as I could find a buyer, change my name and try to forget the whole mess. Obviously I couldn't take my own name again; I was dead. It was a dirty shame, but when I married Sue it would have to be as Pierre LeBourget or Israel Masseltof. I could explain to her that I was switching names for professional purposes.

As I drove along I began to think of what to christen myself. Paul Durant? Nuts, that sounded to phony, even for Hollywood. Richard Taylor? Alexander Gates? Fred Lawson? Bill Todd, maybe? Or Jack P. Garrison? Or how about Archie Robertson? That sounded real enough, because who in the name of Hannah would pick the name Archibald for an alias? But, I don't know. None of them had the kosher ring. They were names you'd find in a book, not a newspaper. For a minute I considered using my real name again—Aaron Rothenberg—which I'd changed almost ten years before at the advice of Professor Puglesi; but I vetoed that as soon as it entered my mind. I was afraid it could be traced. The best bet was to start from scratch. Howard Beldam? Max Allinson....

There were quite a number of fellows hitchhiking along the road but I passed them all by. It wasn't that I didn't want to give them a lift—hell, I was in sympathy—but I just didn't think it was fair having them in the same car with me. If I was picked up, the cops would grab them, too—as accomplices, accessories after the fact, or whatever they wanted to hold them on. Not only that, I was packing a mighty tempting roll. Some dirty crook might make a try for it and I didn't want to hurt anybody. I'd had quite enough excitement for one trip.

But near the airport at Desert Center I pulled up for

water. There was a woman sitting outside the service station, exercising her thumb. Now most smart motorists pass up these female hitchhikers, because usually they're plenty tough and not exactly debutantes from The Four Hundred. They have a reputation for stickups, badgering and blackmail, using the Mann Act as a weapon. But what can a guy expect to find on a public highway? Anyway, this dame, looked O.K. to me—I put her down as just some local kid only going a few miles, maybe into Mecca to see an aunt or her boy friend—so I thought I'd give her a break. "Hop in, sister," I called.

She came running over to the car, carrying a little overnight-case. I opened the door for her, took the bag and slid it on the floor under the dash. There was no sense fooling with the rumble for that tiny thing. She got in and I started up.

"How far are you going?" I asked her. How far are you going? "

That took me by surprise and I turned my head to look her over. She was facing straight ahead so I couldn't see her eyes, but she was young, not more than twenty-four—and dirty. So help me God, I don't think I ever saw a woman as dirty as that in my life. She had on a torn dark dress which hung in wrinkles from her thin body, shoes that were rundown at the heel, and on her legs she wore what had once been a pair of silk hose. Man, she looked as if she'd just been thrown off the crumbiest freight train in the world. About the only clean part about her was her face, which was bare of make-up.

Yet, in spite of the condition she was in, I got the impression of beauty. Not the beauty of a movie actress, or the beauty you dream about when you're in bed with your wife, but a natural beauty, a beauty that's almost homely because it's so damned real. Probably after a bath, an appointment with the hairdresser and wearing a new outfit, she'd look like anyone else you'd meet on the street; but filthy like that and without a mask of cosmetics, she was, I felt, just the kind of woman Adam or Noah or some primitive geezer would have gone for.

Then, suddenly, she turned around to face me and I took it all back. Her mouth and eyes were enough to give a man the jitters. The mouth was stony and thin, almost a slit across her face; and the eyes—well, they might have been pretty if they hadn't had that glassy shine to them, that funny glint I wouldn't even attempt to describe. A peculiar feeling ran over me when I looked into them. It was goofy, but I got the impression there was something behind them, something pretty terrible...

"How far did you say you were going?" she repeated.

Keyed up as I was, almost to the breaking point, I wanted to get her out of the car. I don't know why, but I didn't like her. She made me uneasy and I was nervous enough, I can tell you, without adding to it. But before I knew it the cat was out of the bag and I admitted I was going through to Los Angeles. What I should have told her was I was only going as far as Mecca, and maybe I could have ducked her there. Too late.

"Los Angeles is good enough for me, mister." I was afraid of that.

I kept the car rolling at about forty-five or fifty, no faster. This was California, and that meant speed cops, speed cops and more speed cops. They lay in wait for you in every side road and behind billboards to welcome you to The Land of Eternal Sunshine and to present you with a ticket as a souvenir, the bastards. A friend of mine had tipped me off to this and, since the last thing I wanted at that moment was to get myself pinched, I took it easy.

The girl must have been pretty tired because she fell asleep not twenty minutes after she stepped into the car. She lay sprawled out with her feet on her little overnight-case and her head resting against the far door—like Haskell. I didn't like that part of it much but I didn't wake her up. From the curt replies she had made to my questions, I could see she didn't care to carry on a conversation. Well, when it came to that, neither did I. It wasn't that she still worried me. I'd gotten over that peculiar feeling, which I put down as just my jangled nerves. Nevertheless, I reflected, the less I said to her the better. It has always been my suspicion that half the men in jail today would never have been caught if they had had sense enough to keep their mouths shut. Many a tongue has put a noose around a neck.

Now, with her eyes closed and the tenseness gone out of her lips, she looked harmless enough, almost helpless; and instead of disliking her I began to feel sorry for her. The poor kid probably had had a tough time of it. You could read work—hard work—on her little rough hands with the nails on some of the fingers chewed down to the quick, lack of food on her thin wrists. As far as the rest of her went, you couldn't tell much. Her nose was nice, turned up just a wee bit at the end; her lashes were long and black and genuine; and her breasts were small and high, the way I like breasts to be. But she was too thin and she had practically no hips. For this reason her dress didn't seem to fit.

I kept looking at her out of the corner of my eye for a long time, wondering who she was, why she was going to Los Angeles and where she had come from in the first place. I had asked her all of those questions when she first got in the car, but her answers had all been vague. Her name was Vera, though. I didn't quite catch the last part. Vera's manner puzzled me in a way. She didn't seem at all grateful for the lift I was giving her. She acted as if it was only natural, that it was coming to her. I had half-expected her to go into ecstasies when I told her I was going all the way to the coast. However, when I said I'd take her to Los Angeles, she wasn't at all surprised or pleased. She merely nodded her head and shot me a look I couldn't understand. It was a funny look, shrewd and calculating, and a couple of times I turned my head and caught it again. That gave me the notion that this dame was a little simple upstairs.

But I no longer had that uneasiness. With each mile that went by, my mind was clearing and I was losing that panicky fear of arrest. I knew that the closer I got to Los Angeles, the safer I was. Seeing that I'd missed my breakfast back in Blythe, I was very hungry. I stopped the car in front of an eating place in Mecca and tapped the girl on the shoulder. She opened her eyes, and for a second, while they blinked at the light, they were soft and pale blue. Then, when she saw me leaning over her, I could see them change, become dark and take on that steely glint. She sat up.

"Are you hungry, Vera?" I asked her. Before she could open her mouth to say she was, I knew she was. "O.K. Come on in here and I'll fill your tummy."

Without a word, she opened the door and got out, taking her overnight-case along. That got me hot under the collar: I'm only human. When I do someone a favor I like to be thanked for it, the same as anyone. This Vera had no manners. "Don't you know how to say, 'Thank you'?"

But she didn't answer me. Maybe she didn't hear me.

It was cool in the place—not like Alaska, by any means, but cooler than outside. I took off my coat and hung it on a peg. Vera didn't stop at the table. She went straight back to the Ladies' Room. I was pretty dusty myself, but I let it slide. I didn't like the idea of spending even a minute in the washroom where I couldn't keep an eye on the car outside. I was all set to beat it out the back entrance if a cop went over to it. So I busied myself reading the menu until Vera came back. I was pleased to find she had changed her stockings, combed her hair and put make-up on her face. All cleaned up, she looked like a different person and as much as she got my goat I couldn't help standing up until she was seated.

A waiter shuffled over to the table to take our orders. I glanced at the menu again. Pot roast of beef, brown gravy. Hot veal sandwich with mashed potatoes. Liver and bacon—with onions 5c. extra.... Then my eye lighted on a certain item and a little devil started chuckling in me. I started to smile. I tried but I couldn't resist the temptation. I had to get it out if it killed me.

"Say, Vera. How about a steak?"

She didn't react the way I had hoped. She nodded and turned to the waiter cooly, not like the dame who had bummed a ride, like a god-damned aristocrat.

"Medium rare, please. And for the vegetable, I'll take the corn."

"Coffee now or later?"

"With the dessert."

I was disgusted. I swore up and down that before I did another thing for Vera I'd croak. That's how much I knew.

Vera, Vera. It was just my luck to have picked her up on the highway, just my luck that of all the hundreds of people waving thumbs she happened to be planted in front of the gas station where I pulled in for water. It couldn't have been Mary or Helen; it had to be Vera—the one person I should never have bumped into. But I didn't find that out until we were almost into Riverside. To make conversation, I had been asking her questions every now and then, getting a "no" or occasionally a "yes" in reply. Then, all at once, she turned to me.

"You've been asking me a lot of questions, mister. Now I want to ask you one."

"Go right ahead, Vera," I said, glad that for once she was going to contribute something.

"All right. What I want to know is this: Where did you leave him?"

Maybe you don't believe a man can turn to ice, that its only a figure of speech and nature doesn't function that way? Well, you're wrong, because I did. I got cold all over—my feet, my hands and the rest of me. The shiver shot up my spine so fast it shocked me, catching me with my mouth wide open and my throat so full of heart I almost gagged.

"Where did I *what?*"

"Where did you leave the owner of this car? You're not fooling me. This car belongs to a fellow named Haskell, That's not you, mister."

I fumbled for words, crazy with fear. "You're off your nut. I'm Charles Haskell. Look. I can prove it. Here's my driver's license." I dug into my pockets, feeling for the wallet. She watched me for a second with an amused smirk on her pinched little face.

"Save yourself the trouble, mister," she said at last with a bite to her voice.

"I know you've got Haskell's wallet. I spotted it in the restaurant. But having it doesn't mean a thing—makes it worse, if anything. It just happens I rode with Charlie Haskell all the way from Louisiana. He picked me up outside of Shreveport."

I stared at her, dumbfounded. "You rode with...?"

Then it all came back to me, all that talk about dueling and scars and scratches. In my mind's eyes I could see three mean red lines on Haskell's wrist. I could hear that loud laugh of his....Right on both counts Detroit. I was wrestling with the most dangerous animal in the world. A woman.... I shot a glance at Vera's chewed and ragged nails. Yes, they were capable of doing plenty of damage.... I want to buy some gum and put more iodine on these scratches. They, sting like hell. There ought to be a law against, women with sharp nails. I put her out on her ear.... No, there could be no doubt any more. Vera must be the woman Haskell had spoken, about. She must have passed me while I slept in Blythe.

"Well?"

What was there to say? I kept telling myself to snap into it and think, think! Jeeze, there must be some alibi...

"Well?"

Damn her, she had me dead to rights. There was no use trying to lie my way out of it. With time I probably could have figured out some excuse, but she was keeping after me. It was like hitting a man when he's down. Yes, my goose was cooked. That Haskell son of a bitch wasn't dead yet. He wasn't stretched out stiff and cold, in that Arizona gully; he was sitting right beside me in the car, laughing like hell while he haunted me. My head was whirling.

"Well? Are you tongue-tied? Where did you dump him?"

Slowly it came dribbling out, the whole story, just as it had happened. While I was talking I didn't look at her. I knew in advance she wouldn't believe me and I didn't want to see the scornful twist to her mouth. She interrupted me once or twice by asking a question, but when I got finished she sat in silence. I began to wonder what she intended to do—and what I could possibly do to persuade her to keep her mouth shut. I was aware that the girl sitting next to me, weak, undernourished and scarcely a hundred pounds, wielded a terrible weapon. She could finish me if she chose. I drove along slowly, waiting. It was her move.

IV. SUE HARVEY

I didn't phone the Fleishmeyer Agency; I missed my three o'clock appointment at Paramount and came to work the next afternoon twenty minutes late. The boss was very nice about it though—in the pig's neck. He suggested, in his broken English, that I fix my alarm clock, spend less time in the company of broken down picture actors and deduct a dollar from my weekly pay. But he didn't fire me. He knew what a hard time he would have trying to hire another girl to fit my uniform.

"What I do after hours is my own affair," I told him. "And I'll go out with whomever I please. "

Mr. Bloomberg shrugged his fat shoulders.

"So it's your funeral, not mine. I only try to look after my girls like a father. I don't want to see any of them in trouble. Actors out here you can get a dime a dozen, but good waitresses don't grow on trees. Now, hurry up. That sedan ain't taken care of yet."

My work I did as usual—efficiently but mechanically. My body would be occupied carrying trays, taking orders and calculating checks while my mind would be elsewhere. I was a day-dreamer from the time I went to work until Selma came on to relieve me at midnight. There could be a terrific racket going on around me—dishes clattering, horns blowing and motors roaring—without it distracting me. I was deaf to most of these sounds. When customers addressed me it would register, but little more than just that. The fresh young fellows in huge, expensive cars with empty gas tanks could jolly me all they liked. I never complained because I took no notice of any remarks other than definite orders.

And my dreams? Oh, the usual Hollywood hopes: a contract, some money, stardom and that sort of thing. They were silly, of course; I knew that. Mathematically, I hadn't a chance in a million, Gaynor or no Gaynor. Still, in Hollywood, even the exact science of arithmetic cannot dull the hope, the secret belief even, that you will be the lucky one. Only not entirely lucky. You are talented also, and you are beautiful. The studios only have to awakened to the fact, that is all.

And then sometimes I'd pretend I was on my way back to New York to see my friends. Not as a failure, naturally. I'd step from the train at Grand Central, or from the plane at Newark Airport, dressed in a Paris frock and wearing a chinchilla coat. The press people would all be waiting, armed with flash cameras and note-books. And there would be flowers, offers for personal appearances, a handful of autograph-seekers (not too many to be annoying), and Alex. He would be wearing a new suit of clothes-made-to order, not one of his customary $19.95 specials—and a shirt that wasn't frayed at the collar. He would be shaved and his hair would be neatly cut and his shoes shined. He would know enough to tip the Red-Caps and he would refrain from slapping me on the back and calling me "Sue". I wouldn't be Sue Harvey any more. My name would be Suzanne Harmony... And, oh, yes. There would be several legitimate stage producers at the station, too. They would wave contracts at me and beg me to sign for a role. My answer would have to be: "No, no. I'm sorry, Mr. Harris, Mr. Schubert, Mr. Pemberton. I'm signed on a long-term contract with Metro-Goldwyn-Mayer and I am not permitted to do a play." And perhaps Bellman would be in the crowd and plead with me to come to his club for one night to help business along. My manager would object to this strenuously, but I would overrule him for the sake of old times. "Yes, I'll come, Bellman. Anything to help out a friend." Then the opening night of Thais, in which I would portray the part of a notorious dancer (my past experience would come in handy there). It would be at the Music Hall in Radio City, and there would be kleigs and a long, red carpet and a broadcaster. I would step from a Duesenberg town-car, dressed in a metal-cloth creation which cost three hundred dollars—$299.85, to be exact, including the tax—and Alex would be my escort, in a full-dress suit, if I had to kill him to get him into one....

Stupid? Yes, I suppose so. And funny, when you come to think that I imagined ail this while working in a greasy hamburger-stand. Yet, I believe a goodly number of shop girls, waitresses, models, laundresses and housewives shared these dreams. There are many Garbo and Dietrich scrubbing floors, washing dishes, selling stockings; loads of Barrymores and Taylors and Colemans parking cars.

Occasionally actors or actresses drove in to the stand, sometimes even in costume and with panchromatic smeared on their faces. Although I would pretend indifference, I couldn't help feeling a thrill merely in waiting on them. They were creatures out of the world I was creating, a world more often real to me than reality. Most of them I knew were no more than extras or bit players, yet that sense of importance shrouded them—even if they went away, as so many of them did, without leaving a tip. Producers, directors, writers and technicians were pointed out to me, too. But they were different. Compared with the actors they looked very dull and ordinary.

It was nine-thirty before the dinner rush was over and I had half a minute to sit down, catch my breath and glance at the Examiner. I like to read the gossip columns to see who went where, did what and why. None of that, of course, is any concern of mine; however, it makes me feel that I am keeping in close touch with things. The front pages which deal chiefly with foreign wars, strikes and politics bore me to distraction. Like most Hollywood people, I believe the sun rises over Glendale and sets some place in the neighborhood of Culver City; I don't care particularly who sits down and strikes where, what party holds the reins of government, or whether Senator

So-and-so proposes a bill in Congress or not. Who
Selznick is planning to use in his Gone with the Wind
cast is more in my line. Perhaps this is a very narrow
attitude to take, but the picture industry is the most
important thing in my life. My pet theory is that if only
other people would think more about their occupations
and less about what the Japanese are doing or the
Germans, there would be little unrest in the country. Is
that an idiotic notion? I don't know; maybe it is.

I glanced through a paper one of the customers had
left behind and almost at once my eye fell on a small item
which made my heart leap. FILM PLAYER HURT IN FALL.
I can't understand it. The moment my eye lighted on that
heading I had a feeling it was Raoul. And of course, it
was. He was in the Cedars of Lebanon Hospital with
lacerations and a dislocated arm.

My first reaction upon running across the article was
surprise, naturally; then it became remorse for having
treated the boy so shabbily when it had all been my own
fault. However as I read along, I began to smile. It wasn't
very nice, but I immediately began to think that here was
something else for Raoul to add to his scrapbook. Here
were five full paragraphs dealing with him alone. But the
final paragraph, when I reached it, wiped the smile off my
face:

"The accident, according to the actor, happened
during the course of his morning constitutional, a climb
to the top of the Hollywood mountain. Not far from the
old sign at the peak, he slipped and fell. The brush
growing on the steep sides of the mountain fortunately
broke the fall and saved him from what easily might have
been a fatal injury. Mr. Kildare, last seen as the young
aviator in 'Wings of the Damned' is for the present at
liberty, so his accident will cause no casting difficulties."

I read the article through again for a more definite hint as to what time the accident occurred. Yes, it was a little before seven o'clock. That meant he must have gone up there soon after he had left me at my door. A cold hand began to close over my heart. I was responsible. The more I thought about it the more positive I grew that the mishap had not been a mishap. Try as I might to dismiss the thought, I became convinced that he had taken to heart what I'd said to him and it had made him despondent. For was it reasonable that Raoul should want to climb mountains in the rain? And at that ungodly hour? Even in Hollywood people don't do such silly things, unless they're drunk or surrounded by publicity men. Raoul had been sober as a judge, if that is an accepted simile.

I was worried. Not about Raoul particularly, for he wasn't seriously hurt, but about myself. I suddenly recognized myself to be a weapon, every bit as formidable as a knife or a gun, and liable to do untold damage unless kept in check. Now someone had actually attempted suicide because of a few words I had uttered. I didn't want anything like that to happen and, for the first time in my life, I began to realize just how deadly our tongues can be. I am afraid up until that time I had been in the habit of speaking without thinking, saying things I really didn't mean and not caring a great deal what effect my words took. Scenes came back to me out of the past: Sammie Keener, when I handed him his hat and told him I never wanted to see him again because he was a hopeless drunk; Bellman, when I laughed at his clumsy attempt to make love to me and when I told him to act his age, that he was old enough to be my father; Alex Roth, the time I bawled him out for doing no more than turn on a bed-lamp. Those things all had hurt. God knows how long the sting had lasted. I hadn't given them a thought because I didn't know any better and wasn't there to see the damage. However, now, with Raoul falling or jumping off mountains, I was afforded the privilege of witnessing the whole show. I didn't care for it, I can tell you.

I went inside the stand and telephoned the Cedars, Mr. Kildare was doing very well, thank you—as well as could be expected. Visiting hours were in the afternoon. Yes, I could come in the morning after ten if that was the only time I had free. No, Mr. Kildare could not receive a phone call at that hour. If there was any message I wanted to leave, it would be delivered to him first thing in the morning.

After I hung up I sat there in the booth biting my nails. Was I jumping to conclusions? After all, why should Raoul care one bit what I said about him? I was nothing in his life—just a girl he had been to bed with. But climbing up to the sign, and in the rain, and immediately after seeing me home.... Too much coincidence there. I stepped out of the booth and looked on the counter for the paper. I thought that maybe if I read it again... but someone had walked off with it.

The remainder of the night was ruined for me. Usually the hours went by quickly and Selma's arrival at midnight to relieve me was always something of a surprise. Tonight it was different. Time dragged like nothing human, and I was in such an unpleasant frame of mind that I slapped the short-order cook for a childish prank which at any other time I would have ignored. "What's the matter?" I heard him grumble. "Is it made of gold?"

Selma came to work thirty minutes early. That was quite a shock to everyone. Although she was conscientious and a very good worker and never even so much as a minute late, her appearance at the stand always was on the dot of twelve. You could almost regulate your watch by her. Mr. Bloomberg, who was preparing to go home, nodded in satisfaction—although he took pains to conceal his approval from her by grumbling how terrible business was in answer to her "good evening". Mr. Bloomberg's idea of an employer was somebody who is ill-treated, a scapegoat and a martyr. Had there been any hair on his head, he would have blamed the grey ones on his cooks and waitresses. After Selma had changed into her uniform, she came out to where I was stationed. "You're not off yet, Sue. It's only eleven-forty. I came early so I could talk to you."

There was very little business at that hour so what there was of conversation went uninterrupted. "Did you see the paper?" she asked, coming right to the point.

"Yes. Too bad, wasn't it?"

"Yes. "

"Lucky he wasn't killed. What a fool thing to be doing in the rain."

She fixed a penetrating stare on my face and for what seemed like a long time she didn't say anything. I felt very uncomfortable standing there, with Selma trying to read my mind. I had nothing to conceal, but my eyes felt shifty for all of that. That annoyed me. I made up my mind if she became too inquisitive I'd put her in her place. What had happened between Raoul and me was my business, not hers. Yet, there was something about her which put me on the defensive, an air of authority. I respected it, strangely enough.

"Sue, what did you do to him?"

"Do?"

"Yes. I know something happened. It would take more than just no work to drive Raoul to do thing like that."

"I don't know what you're talking about."

Selma moved closer, so close that I could smell the Dentine on her breath. Her large breasts pressed against my shoulder.

"Oh, yes, you do. You were out with him last night, weren't you?"

"What if I was?"

"You were the last person with him."

"Well? Is that any business of yours?

She hesitated a second. When at length she spoke it was in a calm, quiet voice. It was strange, but I would have felt better if she had shouted.

"Yes, I'm afraid it is. Raoul is... a friend of mine. I've known him for a long time and I wouldn't like to see him wind up wrong."

I didn't relish the implication and I flared into a temper. I don't fly off the handle very often, but this was a deliberate slap in the face. "What's the matter, Selma? Are you jealous because he went out with me instead of taking you out?"

This time it was Selma who dropped her eyes and I knew I'd hit me sore spot. I felt repaid, and with it a generous mood came over me. I would give up Raoul, nobly, like the wife in a movie to "the other woman." Selma could not fail to appreciate the sacrifice... Of course, since I really didn't care about the man it wouldn't hurt very much. But Selma needn't know this. Selma, however, spoiled it all.

"No, I'm not jealous. Nothing of the kind. I don't care how many little tramps Raoul runs around with—providing they're harmless. But I'm not so sure about you, Harvey. You have a mean streak."

Can you imagine such a thing!

No one, not even my mother, had ever spoken that way to me before. A mean streak, indeed! While all my life I may have been thoughtless, I had never been deliberately mean, that I know of. My dander was up. I wanted to fly into her with my nails and rake that sullen look from her face. I don't know what kept me from doing it—unless it was because I realized that was exactly what Selma was hoping to do. Selma was built like a peasant.

"Yes," she continued, "you're hard and mean. I've only known you a few months, but it sticks out all over you. You want to get ahead and you don't care who you step on if you can make the grade. Now Raoul Kildare is a nice boy—too good for your kind. I'm not going to sit by and watch you play him for a sucker. I saw him this afternoon at the hospital. From what I gathered, that fall wasn't an accident. I'm giving you fair warning that...”

I didn't love the man, didn't care whether I ever saw him again or not, but I couldn't let Selma give me “warnings”. I would see Raoul again. I would go out with him, if only to show her I refused to be bossed.

“You mind your own business,” I said through closed teeth. “I'll go out with him whenever I like. And if it burns you up, all the better.”

“You'll be sorry.”

I laughed in her face .

But later that night as I lay in bed alongside of Ewy, I began to consider the things Selma had accused me of being. Was I mean and hard? No, of course I wasn't. What an idea! I was always feeling sorry for someone and doing things for people I didn't really have to do. I want to get ahead, but I was certainly not the ruthless type.

That got me wondering. I began to ask myself what things wouldn't I do to land a contract. A whole flock of things came into my head at first—because I am essentially a decent person, even if I am ambitious. Nevertheless, after I weighed them honestly and balanced them opposite a fat part, they weeded out and the list gradually kept shrinking.

I wouldn't sell my body, of course—or would I? That was a disgusting thought and one I would have preferred to dismiss; but, well, would I or not? The truthful answer: I would. It would be a loathsome ordeal and I would hate every minute of it, but it would be over in no time and there were always some sacrifices a girl must make for the sake of her art. But only if the man was thin and youngish. I can't stand fat men...such as Manny Fleishmeyer.

What else wouldn't I do? There wasn't much, frankly. I was dead earnest about my film career, and the obstacles I would have to encounter did not bother me half as much as the thought that I might never have the opportunity to meet one of them. As yet there was not even a glimmer of hope ahead. In the final analysis, about the only thing I most certainly would not do was kill someone.

But that did not necessarily imply I was stepping on anyone by going out with Raoul—except poor Alex, who, after all, knew nothing about it. Raoul in no way affected my intended career. He wasn't a big enough figure to be able to help me. Good night, the way Selma talked one would think he was a star or an important executive, instead of a mere bit-player! All that threw me off on to the subject of Mr. Kildare. I commenced to wonder what he was thinking of the whole thing. Had he mentioned me to Selma when she visited him? Was he very angry? Was he injured—his pride, I mean? Was he in love with Selma? She with him? Or he with me? It was rather amusing to consider how very little I knew about the man who had attempted to kill himself because of me. I knew his name. But that was about all.

This business about being in love with me: I hadn't taken it into consideration before. While loads of men at one time or another have fallen in love with me—chiefly because I wanted them to—Raoul had displayed no visible sign that he was smitten. I remembered his attitude and grew a little provoked. I decided he was too conceited to care anything about anyone except himself. He was the kind who told a girl "I love you" just to hear the sound of his voice; and when she believed him and he got his way he went home later on and patted himself on the back, thinking what a great lover he was and how Casanova could have learned plenty from him.

There are a great many men like that. However, sometimes they get caught in their own trap. They try to be so convincing in their lives that they finally succeeded in convincing even themselves; and when eventually they wake up they are either married or in trouble. As for myself, I am also of the type easily carried away by props, dialogue and special effects. If there is a romantic background, a handsome man with a good line, and nothing to distract me—like phones ringing or magazine salesmen coming to the door—I'm apt to think I'm in love. The feeling only lasts momentarily, but very often that moment or two is all the fellow needs. I wish I had been made differently.

However, with Raoul I never for an instant fancied myself in love. He had made no effort to woo me that way. It had been straightforward sex, brought about by a quantity of inferior rye which he had fed me as rapidly as I could down it. There had been no lies, however sweet to hear, nothing at all to which I could cling later as an excuse for what we did. The man hadn't even tried to persuade me with the wild, Hollywoodish philosophy, stolen from the Rubaiyat and translated into slang. He had gone about the task of seducing me as simply and as matter-of-factly as a surgeon taking out a patient's tonsils. The thing that puzzled me though was why the patient hadn't struggled.

But mat was beside the point. It had nothing to do with the grave issue at hand. Since I am a believer in that old adage about burying the past before it buries you, I wanted to wash my hands of the whole affair. But first there was a lot to be ironed out. I couldn't go on and let the poor devil kill himself because of anything to do with me. Fun is fun. It ends there.

So at the risk of having him refuse to see me, I made up my mind to go to the hospital in the morning. I'd go early, to avoid running into Selma. I wasn't afraid of her in any sense of the word—I just didn't like her—but running into her might cause a scene. I'd bring some flowers along with me too, as a peace offering. I'd scrape together a few dollars for carnations or chrysanthemums and to hell with mother this week. Mother could wear her fall suit a little while longer. Raoul was far more important at the moment. He was probably in pain. While it wasn't exactly my fault that he was suffering (he was a grown man and if he wanted to be crazy it was his business), I felt somewhat guilty Selma had guessed that much correctly.

This settled, I poked Ewy in the ribs. I hated to awaken her, but I never hear alarms when I want to hear them. She sat up in bed.

"Now what?"

"Oh, are you awake, Ewy?"

"I wasn't, until you jabbed your fist into me!"

"Did I? Oh, I'm sorry. Go back to sleep, honey. I'll be careful next time I rollover ."

"See that you do. My god, have a little consideration!"

"Well, no sense getting angry about it. I said I was sorry, didn't I?"

"All right. Only shut up."

"Good night."

"Umm."

"And Ewy..."

"Well, what is it now?"

"Will you get me up when you leave for work tomorrow?"

"I'll do my best. Good night."

"Be sure I get up, will you? It's important."

"All right."

"Well, good night, Ewy. Sleep tight."

She didn't answer me.

Even after having made that decision I tossed around in bed for hours. I made three not-very-necessary trips to the bathroom, reading a fifteen minute Liberty story and a short note from Ewy to the effect that Mr. Fleishmeyer called and wanted to know if I had died, and that due to a horse named Black Brigand, Ewy would be two dollars short on the grocery fund this week. I felt uneasy in my mind and I kept seeing Raoul's face before me. At one moment he would be kissing me and, at the next, balancing himself on top of one of the letters in the sign H-O-L-L-Y-W-O-O-D. I caught myself spelling the word over and over again. H-O-L-L-Y-W-O-O-D. It didn't put me to sleep, like counting sheep jumping over a fence; it kept me awake. At length I sat up and felt on the night-table for my package of cigarettes. Lighting one, I held the match close to the battered face of the clock on the floor beside the bed. It was four-thirteen. I propped the pillow up behind my back, drew the covers under my knees and sat there smoking until dawn. I just couldn't sleep.

It is going to be extremely difficult to describe my visit to the hospital the next day. This is because the whole thing remains vague to me. I found out two things which absolutely astonished me, so for the greater part of the half hour I was in a fog. When I finally came out of the place I crossed Fountain Avenue and looked for the nearest bar. I needed a drink and needed one badly. For not only did I find out what was going on in Raoul's mind, I found out what was hidden in mine.

It will always remain a mystery to me: how we can go along blissfully from day to day, never realizing things which have happened to us. Why we can't detect feelings that are new without having the roof fall in suddenly is the craziest unanswerable question of nature. Have you ever been surprised at yourself? It is a funny feeling. We are so sure we know our inner selves, yet very often we are quite different. Sometimes I think that other people—even comparative strangers—know us better than we know ourselves. But all this must sound silly. I'll try to relate what happened.

When a nurse ushered me into his room he was sitting up in bed, reading a book. He looked a mess, all right. His head was swathed in bandages and his left arm was in splints. All a person could see of his face was the small area from his mouth to his eyebrows, the rest was gauze and adhesive. The nurse left us alone, for which I was grateful. I didn't know how he would receive me; if he threw the book at me it was just as well we had no audience.

"Hello, Raoul. I... I heard you had an accident and.... well, I've come to see how you are getting along. I... I was passing in the neighborhood so I thought... er...”

I was frightfully uncomfortable. There didn't seem anything to say. His head was still facing front and he had not dropped the book, but even so his eyes were on me. He didn't have to speak. I saw quite clearly that he was greatly surprised to see me, then annoyed, and then ashamed. The visible portion of his face grew as red as his lips.

I came over to the bedside, holding out my hand. Slowly, he lifted his good arm and shook it. I don't know which one of us had the wet palm but I suspect it was me. Yes, he was suffering—but so was I, and every bit as much. All he was facing was a woman who had insulted his manhood; I was facing an over-sensitive boy I had almost killed. I was frightened and embarrassed and at a total loss where to begin to rectify things. The point had been reached where I could no longer pooh-pooh the notion that what he had attempted was due to quite another matter. Everything indicated I was to blame.

“How are you feeling?”

“Oh, I'm all right.”

“You're not in pain?”

“No not much.”

“Is your arm broken?”

“Just dislocated.”

I was feeding him lines, like in a play, anyone of which might be the cue for his replying, “What do you care, you selfish bitch?” I half expected to hear that each time he opened his mouth.

Just then the nurse entered with a vase and arranged my flowers in water. “Aren't they beautiful, Mr. Kildare?” she asked, taking them over to a little table by the side of the bed. Raoul looked at them absently for a moment; I don't believe he even saw them.

“Yes. Very. Thanks.”

“Oh, it's nothing. When do you imagine they'll let you go home?”

“Home?”

"Yes, of course."

"Oh, I don't know. In a few days. Maybe a week."

We both fell silent and there was a tension you could all but hear. I began to fidget with my gloves, my bag and a thread that was loose on his bedspread. Although we were facing each other our eyes did not meet. What, I asked myself, could a person say in a situation like this? I was wishing I hadn't come. If only he would get on his high horse, curse at me and demand an apology it would be a relief. Or if only he took revenge by commenting upon my qualifications in the dark! But no. He sat there saying nothing, looking whipped and very ill at ease.

"You're looking well," I said, when I couldn't stand it any longer. I didn't realize how ridiculous that remark was until later. There he was in a hospital, literally covered with bandages!

"Thanks. You're looking well yourself."

"Thanks. "

"Not at all."

Another long silence. The noises of the hospital crashed in my ears and I decided then and there that no sound is louder and more disturbing than that of persons taking pains to be quiet. Then, suddenly driven to make conversation, we both started to say something at once. Then we both stopped and politely waited. God, it was terrible. In desperation and before a series of you-first-my-dear-Alphonse could commence, I held out my hand. "I've really got to run along now, Raoul. I'm on my way to an appointment. Just thought I'd stop by and tell you I am sorry for what I said the other night. I didn't mean it, of course. I must have been high."

He didn't flush this time. He merely dropped his eyes.

"Oh, that's all right. It doesn't matter now."

There was a hopelessness in his voice that worried me no end. Was he going to try it over again when he got discharged from the hospital? He answered that question himself a second later in reply to my, "Well, I hope I'll see you again very soon."

"I don't think it's likely. I expect to leave for New York immediately. I have a chance for a nice part in the new Harris production that's going into rehearsal this month."

I can't begin to tell you how relieved I was to hear that. At once all nervousness left me and I came back to his bedside from the door. "But that's marvelous, Raoul! It's a break to work for Harris. He's the biggest man on Broadway."

"Oh, I haven't got it yet. I'm only going on spec."

"You'll get it, all right," I said encouragingly. "I've seen your work. You've got loads of talent."

He thanked me quietly, but as though I had only told him something he already knew. However, the attitude was empty. Every trace of conceit and his former armor of braggadocio had vanished in him; a person could scarcely recognize Raoul Kildare in the meek, easily embarrassed figure on the bed. If my words had stripped him of his manhood, they had also taken his self-confidence and his poise. I realized instinctively that my brief apology would never restore all this. The only thing to do was to get to the bottom of it.

"Raoul," I said, despite the fact that I have always been one never to arouse the sleeping dogs, "will you tell me why..."

"Yes?" His voice came as a dare.

"Why you did it?"

He frowned in displeasure for a minute. Then, as his face cleared, I saw the answer. You can see those things, you know—if you'll only look. But what was immediately so plain almost floored me, and inside my head everything became hopelessly jumbled. I dropped my bag on the floor, stooped, picked it up, and then I dropped it again. I was that flustered.

"You don't..." Then it broke, like Niagara. "All right. Now you know. You weren't satisfied before. You had to come sneaking around here to find out more. Why can't you let me alone? Haven't you done enough harm? Now get the hell out of here. Get out, God damn you!"

I leaned over and kissed him on the cheek. He stopped shouting but I could feel his face trembling under my lips. From beneath the bandages covering his forehead a thin trickle of blood commenced to trace a path to his brow. I was completely shaken. "It's all right, Raoul," I heard myself say. It's all right, I love you, too."

Did I or didn't I? That was one whale of a question and I tried to answer it honestly over four Scotch-and-sodas. If I didn't, what was that feeling I had, that warm, enervating glow that made me want to cry? I knew—and there was no sense trying to deny it—that if it had been possible he could have had me right men and there in the hospital. I shouldn't have been able to stop him—not that I would have wanted him to stop. Something about his love struck a responding chord in me. Yes, he did love me. I knew it—certainly much better than I knew my own feelings. How could I be so positive? How did I know he wasn't just acting? That I can't tell you. I just knew.

On the other hand, if I was in love with him, how could I explain Alex? That was the rub as Hamlet would say. Without Alex there would have been not the slightest doubt in my mind; I would have surrendered myself to the fact that I loved Raoul and been done with it. But I loved Alex, too. Is it possible for a person to be in love with more than one man at a time? It never happens in the movies or in The Saturday Evening Post.

With my fourth drink in front of me I commenced to balance the two men, one against the other. In many ways they were much alike. Both of them possessed that "little boy" quality, that air of not being able to care for himself, sort of an innocence, which both took great pains to hide. Alex concealed his beneath an easily cracked shell of cynicism; Raoul, beneath a ridiculous

and actually nonexistent conceit. Men do not like to
think themselves soft. They believe it is unmanly. They
don't realize that a woman can usually see through
whatever pose they strike. Physically, of course, Raoul
and Alex were in different classes. Raoul was handsome
while Alex looked like something the cat dragged in. Yet,
when a person knew Alex and liked him, his face did not
seem to matter. Not that he was very ugly; he wasn't. He
was just plain. It was only when you compared him with
somebody like Raoul that he seemed a mess. Then you
would begin to consider things that had never struck you
before: his ill-fitting suits and the careless way he let his
socks hang, the months he'd go without a haircut and
the days without shaving. Raoul would never have
dreamed of going about like that. But then, I
remembered, Raoul was an actor. It is far more
important for an actor to look well than for a musician.
As a matter of fact, musicians are always sloppy by
tradition.

But when it came to talent, I had to hand it to Alex. I
had seen Raoul in several pictures and what little he had
to do he did well; however, in no way could he approach
the genius of Alex when he had a fiddle under his chin. I
don't care much for highbrow music—maybe because I
don't understand it sufficiently to appreciate it—but I'll
never forget how he could stir me at times just by laying
on his back and going to town on his violin.

After the club, when I invariably was tired and my
head ached (to say nothing of my feet), I'd stretch out
beside him on the bed with my eyes closed and he would
play me to sleep. I never knew what the numbers were. I
think most of the time he improvised. They were soft and
of a pattern, yet, somehow, they didn't seem to have a
tune. Surely, without even knowing the man, anyone
could tell he was neither hard nor cynical. Very often
after he had played for a little while, my headaches left
me and either I fell asleep at once or gradually got the
urge to take him in my arms. He was never rough in

such things—which was more than I could say for Raoul.

Sleeping with Raoul was an adventure, impossible to experience without a great deal of wear and tear on the emotions; with Alex it was accomplished so gently and tenderly that after it was over you scarcely could believe it had happened.

Which one of them did I love?

Even after all this went through my mind I was still as much in the dark as before. I tried to imagine them standing one beside the other against a wall. They were going to be shot at dawn or something. I had the choice of saving one of them... After minutes of reaching out first to one and then the other, the only decision I arrived at was that I needed another drink. I downed my fifth Scotch in a dither.

Raoul needed me most, naturally. He had problems, he was over-sensitive and his career was not going the way he had planned. When a film actor has to travel all the way to New York on spec, work must be scarce and hope pretty low. In that sense, Raoul and I were very much alike and I could understand him. Alex was different. He had no worries, no grave problems. All he had to do was apply to any bandleader and sign the salary list. He didn't need help from anybody.

After the seventh drink it was time to leave for the drive-in. I took a cab, recklessly throwing away a hard-earned seventy cents. How I arrived there and how I managed to get through the night I'll never know. I was just beginning to sober up when Selma came on at midnight to relieve me. She didn't say anything to me when she took up her post, but after I had changed and came out of the dressing-room she told me the boss wanted to see me.

"I can't have drunks working for me," Mr. Bloomberg said when I asked him what he wanted. "This is your last week. I'm sorry."

I don't think I would have suspected anyone's fine Italian hand if I hadn't noticed Selma grinning like a fool,

on my way out. I knew then that she had tattled to
Bloomberg. At any other time I might have been furious,
but that night, with Raoul and Alex on my mind, it didn't
seem to make much difference.

   Yes, Raoul needed me more. If I wasn't sure then, I
was sure when I arrived home. For when I opened the
door to the bungalow, Ewy was sitting in the living-room
waiting up for me. She was crying as she told me Alex
was dead.

V. ALEXANDER ROTH

If there is any worse spot than for a man to find himself a slave to a woman's whims I'd like to know about it. What makes it so tough is you never can be sure what a woman will do. At one moment she's calm and everything is velvet; then, in a flash, it all explodes sky-high and she's got it in for you. And when she's got it in for you, brother, look out. There are never any halfway measures. A woman loves or she hates. Pity and all the feelings in between she never even heard of.

Now you men won't believe this. You were brought up by your mothers to kiss the ladies' hands, to watch your language in their company, to be gentle with them and to realize and appreciate how noble and soft and superior they are.

You were taught from the cradle that men are the hard ones, the roughnecks; and maybe sometimes you wonder why in God's name women have anything to do with us, why they condescend to marry us, to live with us, much less to give in to us.

I used to wonder myself. But that was before all this happened. I can see now that like the lions and the spiders and the snakes, the female human is more vicious than the male. That must be the reason why nobody likes women on juries. If Christ Himself was being tried again, with Liebowitz defending Him, you'd never know what verdict a jury of women would return. Yes, all women are dangerous—and this Vera was no exception. No siree, I should say she wasn't. Vera was like a frozen stick of dynamite; you never knew when she was going to blow.

If a person could believe her, here was a dame who'd touched bottom, who'd been batted around for five or six years from one job to another until she was groggy. She'd been a movie usher in Pittsburgh, a shoe-worker in Binghamton, a cashier in Trenton and God knows what else. She'd washed dishes, scrubbed floors, picked pockets, rolled cigars; she'd lived with cops, clerks, floor-walkers, and every brand of visiting Elk imaginable. Also, she'd kept Haskell's bed warm from Shreveport to El Paso. She'd reached the stage where she hated men and when I say hated, I mean hated—almost as much as she hated women. That little girl was just a bundle of hate.

But she wasn't going to turn me in. "It won't do me any good, having you pinched," she said. "The cops are no friends of mine. If there was a reward... but there isn't."

"Gee, thanks, Vera."

She laughed, like the Romans must have laughed when they saw some poor Carthaginian slob being mangled by a dozen lions. "Oh, don't thank me yet, brother. I'm not done with you by a long shot. Let's see that wallet."

I handed it over and she helped herself to the wad of bills. It broke my heart to see my newly acquired fortune disappear into the top of her stocking, but I didn't holler murder. She had me by that well-known place. If only she'd keep her trap buttoned up she was welcome to the money.

"Is that all Haskell had?"

"Isn't it enough?"

"I thought he had more."

"Not that I know of. You can search me if you think I'm holding out on you."

"Well, maybe I will at that. He told me he was going to bet three thousand dollars on Paradisaical in the fourth at Belmont."

"He must've been stringing you. He meant three hundred."

"Maybe."

"Sure, three hundred; or three bucks. He was a piece of cheese. Big blowhard."

"Listen, mister. Don't try to tell me anything about Charlie Haskell. I knew him better than you did."

"Yeah? Then you know he smoked the weed. That explains his three grand bet."

"I'm not so sure he didn't have that three grand. Why should I believe you? You've got all the earmarks of a cheap crook."

"Now wait a minute—" Yes, she had me. But it went against the grain, having a woman of that caliber tell me the score.

"Shut up. You're a cheap crook and you killed him. For two cents I'd change my mind and turn you in. I don't like you."

She didn't a appear to be bluffing and I was frightened. Those eyes of hers were cold. She wasn't playing poker.

"All right, all right. Don't get sore, Vera."

"I'm not sore. But just remember who's boss around here. If you shut up and don't give me any arguments you have nothing to worry about. If you act wise... well, mister, you'll pop into the can so fast it'll make your ears sing. "

"I'm not arguing, Vera."

"See that you don't. Crooked as you look, I'd hate to see a fellow young as you wind up sniffing that perfume Arizona hands out free to murderers."

"I'm not a murderer."

She gave me one of those sandpapery laughs of hers.

"Of course you're not. Haskell knocked his own head off."

"He fell. That's how it happened. Just like I told you."

"And then he made you a present of his belongings. "

"Aw, I explained why I had to—"

"Oh, skip it," she cut in on me. "It doesn't make any difference one way or another. I'm not a mourner. I liked Haskell even less than I like you."

"Yeah. I saw what you did to him."

"What do you mean by that?"

"Those scratches."

"Oh, sure. I scratched him."

"I'll say you did."

"Well, you give a guy an inch."

We were coming into Pasadena by that time and the traffic was so heavy I had to concentrate on my driving. It was a pretty town, all right; but I wasn't enjoying it. I was experiencing a feeling I hadn't had in almost twenty years: that leaden sensation I got when I was smoking a cigar in the bathroom and my father walked in.

"Pull in to the curb in front of that drug store," Vera commanded. "I want to get a pint."

I pulled in.

"No, park the car and come in with me."

"This is a Bus Stop, Vera. You run in. Then if a cop comes I can move."

"Nothing doing. You're coming in, too. From now on you and I are the Siamese Twins. Drive around the corner if you think we'll get a tag."

I shrugged. It was too hot to argue. "Have it your own way. But I don't get the point."

Vera got sarcastic. "The point is I don't want you to get lost."

"I'm not going to beat it, if that's what you're afraid of."

"I'll say you're not. I want the dough we're going to make on this car."

"That's O.K. by me. But what then? After we sell it can I go?"

"After we sell it we'll see."

I parked the Buick two blocks away and we walked back to the pharmacy together. Vera bought two pints of Ten High, a carton of Chesties and a pair of sun-glasses. She also got some cosmetics—cold creams, vanishing creams, tissue creams and that sort of truck. The bill came to more than seven bucks. When I asked her to buy me a pair of sun-glasses too, she squawked.

"But I broke the pair I had and I can't see to drive without them, Vera," I said. "Jeeze, what's a pair of fifteen cent glasses to you?"

"You're a pest," she snapped. "Here."

I forgot to say thanks on purpose. Half an hour later we rolled down the Los Feliz hill to Western Avenue, then drove along Hollywood Boulevard to Vine.

There I recognized places Sue had written me about: Tip's, The Brown Derby, The Coco Tree, Eddy Cantor's, the Broadway, the hock shop off Selma, the Plaza Hotel. Down the Boulevard a neon sign kept spelling: ALL ROADS LEAD TO HOLLYWOOD—AND THE PAUSE THAT REFRESHES—DRINK COCA COLA. What a joke. That sign should have read: ALL ROADS LEAD TO HOLLYWOOD—AND THE COUNTY JAIL—DRINK POISON. When I got to thinking about all that had happened to me on the way, things I hadn't planned in my itinerary, I began to wonder if it was worth it. Two month's of hell-hitching rides, going without meals, sitting in a cell, becoming involved in a death, and now at the mercy of a female tramp—for what? I was just coming to the conclusion that men are mere debris in the gale Fate whips up, and that when they make future plans they are fools. My own case is a corking example. Was it Shakespeare, Robert Burns or Ralph Waldo Emerson who wrote, "The best laid plans of mice and men often go blooey"? Well, whoever it was said a mouthful.

"Anyway, I'm here," I said aloud.

"You mean 'we', don't you?" commented Vera, than she started to laugh.

Ha, ha. It was very funny.

I soon found out Vera wasn't kidding about that Siamese Twins crack, for we rented a small apartment on

Afton Place as Mr. and Mrs. Charles Haskell. When I objected to this, she explained that it was on account of the car. A dealer might smell a mouse if he called and found out we were using another name, and it was important that the business be transacted strictly according to Holy.

The place only had one bedroom, so it was yours truly for the couch. I took one of the pillows from the bed, a blanket and a sheet. I wasn't exactly sleepy, but I thought I'd catch a nap while Vera was in the shower. I don't know how long I dozed, but when I opened my eyes again I was stiff and sore and I let loose some choice profanity before I noticed Vera standing beside the couch, grinning down at me.

"That couch isn't so hot, is it, Roth?"

"The Spanish had worse. Only they had spikes in theirs. And they called them racks, not davenports. "

"I feel sorry for you," she said sarcastically.

"Say, why don't you take off your clothes when you go to bed? Or is it a habit you got into in jail?"

"Go to hell," I said.

Then I noticed she had on Haskell's woolly bathrobe. "It's tough Haskell wasn't a woman," I observed, "so you could use what's in the suit-case."

"Oh, I've decided to let you keep that stuff—except the suits. They ought to bring a sawbuck apiece in a hock shop. I just came out to tell you I'm finished with the shower, if you want to use it."

"Thanks. "

"Your towel is the one with the blue border."

I took a pair of Haskell's pyjamas into the bathroom with me and stayed under the shower a long time. When I finally came back into the living-room Vera was sitting on the couch smoking a cigarette and sipping a drink. She had taken off Haskell's robe. All she was wearing was a pair of his silk pyjamas with the sleeves rolled up.

"Have a drink?"

"Aren't you afraid I'll take you up on it?"

"If I didn't want to give you a drink I wouldn't have offered it. Why be a sore-head, Ross? You got yourself into this thing. I didn't. You should be grateful I'm not turning you in. Why, if I wasn't regular, you'd be in the pen this minute being photographed and finger-printed and pushed around by the dicks. So cheer up. Get rid of that long puss. Or is your conscience bothering you?"

"No, it isn't," I replied hotly.

"Fine. That's the spirit. He's dead and no moaning around will bring him back. I never could understand this worrying about something that was over and done with."

"Listen, Vera. For the last time, I didn't kill him."

"All right. If it'll make you sociable, you didn't kill him. Have a drink."

I let her pour me a whisky, the first one for me in three or four months. Then she gave me another. In a couple of hours we killed the two pints. The liquor didn't make me feel any better, but I began to see Vera was right. She hadn't gotten me into this thing. She just happened along to top it off. However, I wasn't to blame either. When I crooked my thumb I was only asking for a lift; I had neither the desire nor the intention to steal the man's car, his clothes, his money and his identity. Those things had all been shoved down me, like castor oil. Like a prize chump, all I'd figured on was three thousand miles of highway separating me from Hollywood and Sue. I didn't count on someone kicking off just at the moment it would look the worst.

Yes, I was feeling sorry for myself—why not? I was getting a raw deal all around. If I had asked for trouble by knocking Mr. Haskell over the head, there would have been no complaints; but who had I ever harmed? All I asked of life was to be left alone, to be allowed to go about my business playing my fiddle.

There must be something wrong with the world. Isn't there any justice, any God? Or is He just a sadistic puppeteer, parked on a throne out of sight, amusing

Himself by jerking the wrong strings? Clear it up for me, someone. Here I was, facing a death penalty, liable to wind up in a station house at any minute, when I hadn't done anything anyone else wouldn't have done. I wasn't to blame. Something or someone might be; but not me, and not Haskell, and not Vera.

However, the realization that Vera was not to blame didn't make me like her more. She was the type of woman I have always despised: the kind who knows all the answers and who makes no bones about being hard-boiled. Even though I know just how women are underneath, I still prefer them to have that phony sweetness in their manner. You know, Sadie Thompson pulling a Ramona. She looked pretty cute in those big pyjamas, and now she was all fixed up with the junk she'd bought in Pasadena; yet, somehow, she didn't seem to be feminine. I guess her truck-drivers vocabulary ruined the illusion.

"We're out of liquor, Roth."

"Yeah."

"Too bad. I felt like getting tight tonight."

"Well, I think you succeeded."

"Am I tight?"

"As a prima donna's corset."

"That's nice. I wanted to get tight."

"Why? What have you to get tight about?"

"Oh, I don't know. Things."

"Nuts. You should have my worries."

"If I had your worries, I'd stay sober."

"Yeah. Maybe you're right."

"I'm always right."

"Sure."

"I don't like the way you say that, mister."

"Well, there's a lot of things I don't like."

"I know. But life is ball game. You have to take a swing at whatever comes along before you wake up and find you're struck out."

"I bet you read that somewhere."

Vera frowned an instant and then decided not to get angry.

"That's the trouble with you, Roth. All you do is bellyache, instead of taking it easy and trying to make the best of things. Why, you're lucky just to be alive! Suppose Haskell had opened that door? You'd be playing a harp now. Think of that."

"You think of it. I'm tired of thinking."

"There's plenty of people dying this minute that would give anything to trade places with you. I know what I'm talking about."

"I'm not so sure. At least they know they're done for. They don't have to sweat blood wondering if they are."

"Your philosophy stinks, mister. We all know we're going to die some day. It's only a question of when. But what got us off on this, anyway? We'll be discussing politics next."

"Or spiritualism. Where did you hide the butts?"

"On the table, sucker."

We bored each other with conversation for about an hour longer, every five minutes one of us wishing we had another pint or a radio or something to read. Then, when we finally ran out of chatter, I suggested the hay. "I know it's only nine o'clock. But we want to get up early and make the rounds of used-car lots."

"No hurry about that. We've got all the time in the world."

"Yeah, maybe you have. But if you think I want to stay cooped up in this place any longer than I have to, you're batty."

"It's not a bad place. You'd pay plenty for diggings like this in New York."

"I wouldn't care if it was the Ritz."

As I said that, I was looking out the window. Somewhere out in the night was Cheremoya Avenue. I didn't have any idea if it was north, south, east or west. I knew it was at the foot of some mountains, that was all. Well, wherever it was, Sue was there sleeping, not dreaming I was nearby. I could see her in her bed, the covers tucked up under her chin and wrapped around her knees the way she liked. If it was a double bed, I really pitied her room-mate. I remembered all the colds I'd caught, waking up in mid-winter without a blanket. Of course when you're in love you don't mind those things. I would gladly have come down with pneumonia before disturbing her.

Vera suddenly had a fit of coughing and I turned away from the window sadly. Her face was red as a beet and she signaled me frantically to get her a drink of water. The spell lasted a full five minutes and when it was done she lay back on the couch, exhausted.

"That lousy liquor," she explained.

"That's a mean cough. You ought to do something about it."

"Oh, I'll be all right."

"That's what Camille said before they patted her with a spade."

"Who?"

"Oh, nobody you know."

"Anyway, wouldn't it be a break for you if I did kick off? You'd be free—and with all that dough and the car."

"I don't want to see anybody die."

"Not even me?"

"Especially not you. One guy died on me. If you did—well, that's all I need."

Vera looked at me closely for a minute. "You don't like me, do you, Roth?"

"Oh, it's not that, Vera," I said, deciding it was better to keep her in a good mood than to tell the truth. "I just hate being a prisoner. When I want to go someplace, I want to go."

"So do I. But we can't always do what we want to do. I'd like to lay my hands on a million. Is that why you're so grouchy?"

"Sure." Better not mention Sue, I cautioned myself. The less Vera knew about me, the less chance she'd have of finding me if I copped a sneak. "That's enough to make anyone feel bad. "

"Well, I'm a good sport. It's still early. If you want us to go out for awhile, how about a movie?"

"I don't feel that bad."

She shrugged her shoulders indifferently. "Have it your own way. God, it's stuffy in here. Open that window."

"It is open."

"I *must be* tight."

And here she got to her feet and began pacing the floor. I watched her in admiration. I couldn't help it. She was one of the most graceful women I'd ever seen. Barefooted and wearing those silk pyjamas that outlined her wiry body, she was like some pantheress, caged and nervous. As she walked, the jacket of Haskell's pyjamas, which she had wrapped around herself, fell open. I turned my head away, but not before I caught a flash of her torso, jutting ribs, small breasts, navel and the rest. She must have been aware of it, but she took her time covering up.

"Hey, what goes on?" I said.

"Does it bother you, Boy Scout?"

"It doesn't bother me. But remember where you are. Aren't you afraid...?"

"Of you? Don't be silly. All you can do is rape me."

All I could do was rape her. Nice talk. The more I was with her, the more the woman disgusted me. It wasn't that she was ugly or anything; it was just her attitude.

"I was thinking of the neighbors. They'll be calling the cops the first thing you know. This isn't Minsky's."

"I'm going to bed. Good night, Roth. Don't try to sneak off during the night, because it won't do you any good. You can't get that chain off the door without making a lot of noise and I'm a light sleeper. Anyway, if I find you gone I'll notify the cops and they'll pick you up on a general alarm."

"Don't worry. I know when I'm in a spot."

"And I've got the car keys, too."

"O.K. Why not take all the pants out of the bag and stuff them under the pillow while you're at it?"

"Good idea."

And, believe it or not, that's exactly what she did. "Well, good night." She went to the bedroom door and paused with her hand on the knob. "I hope you won't be too uncomfortable on the couch."

"Don't lose any sleep over it, will you, Vera?"

"You... you don't have to sleep on that couch, if you don't want to."

Something told me that was coming. Well, to hell with her. She could make me stay put in the apartment. She could make me give her all my dough. She could make me peddle a hot car for her. But there was one thing she couldn't make me do.

"That's all right. I like the couch." I saw her stiffen a little. Then she walked into the bedroom without another word. "Good night, Vera," I called after her.

Later on that night I got to thinking about Sue again, and how I missed her and how much I loved her. The moonlight streamed in through the open window like golden fingers slipping into black gloves. All the objects in the room took on a fairylike quality. They flashed with reflected light. The evening noises blended together into an unearthly music which stimulated me and made the blood course through my veins at a maddening pace. Before my eyes I beheld a vision: an amber body writhing in the dimness, beautiful and frightening at the same time, the personification of Venus, of Bacchus, of unutterable fleshly delights. The sound of drums commenced to pound and pulse in my ears, growing louder until it drowned out everything else. Faster beat the drums, my heart keeping time. I felt feverish, drugged by the pitch, the timbre, the sheer savagery of it all. Taut and tense like the carrying notes of a violin, my senses sprang into being and overwhelmed me....

Isn't that some description? I got it out of a book. But here's something I didn't get out of a book: I wanted Sue so much that night, I went into the bedroom and had Vera. There's reality for you. Go out and roll in it.

If this were a movie, I would fall in love with Vera, marry her and make a decent woman of her. Or else she'd make some supreme Class A sacrifice for me and die, leaving me free to marry Sue. She would experience a complete and totally unwarranted change of heart, wipe out her sins by a dramatic death, pleasing me, the Hays office and the morons in the mezzanine. Sue and I would bawl a little over her grave, make some crack about there is good in all of us and fade out. But this isn't a movie, and Vera, unfortunately, was just as lousy in the morning as she'd been the night before.

Sorry.

You know, it would be a great thing if our lives could be arranged like a movie plot. M.G.M. does a much better job of running humanity than God. On the screen the good people always come out all right in the end. The hero winds up with the girl, a fine position paying forty-nine thousand dollars a week and a medal for bravery into the bargain. No matter how black things look for him in the second reel, before the trap is sprung or the switch is pulled a pardon arrives from the Governor or new evidence is brought in.

And in a movie, if the hero decides to become a doctor, he becomes a doctor, not a grocer or dentist. If he decides to go to Frisco, he goes to Frisco. He doesn't wind up in Miami or New Orleans or in jail. Things are plotted in straight lines. There are never any unexpected happenings which change everything about the hero but his underwear.

Whether people's hopes are the result of pictures or
pictures are based on hopes, I can't say. However, in real
life, things rarely happen so conveniently. The trap is
sprung, and it is a week, a month or a year before the
authorities find out a man is innocent.

Anyway, people still hope, no matter how many
times they see Right unrewarded. And I was no
exception. I was still praying to my own private gods that
within a short time all would be straightened out
satisfactorily. For that reason I woke Vera early and
made such a racket getting dressed that she couldn't go
back to sleep.

"The dealers will still be there in an hour," she
grumbled.

"What time is it, anyway?"

I looked at Haskell's watch which Vera had laid on
the dresser. "Almost eight-thirty. Let's get going."

"Almost eight-thirty! The middle of the night!"

After breakfasting on some of the canned goods
Haskell had in the rumble, we drove around town trying
to interest someone in the car. From the first, Hollywood
appealed to me. Everything looked so clean in the
sunlight. I decided at once that those stories about
people starving to death were exaggerations. The things
that went hand in hand with misery—the ugly
brownstones; the slum sections, the squalor were absent
out here. Palm trees lined the curbs, not the traditional
New York City garbage cans. Besides, the people all
looked so healthy and tanned.

The first dealer we approached owned a lot on Santa
Monica Boulevard, near La Brea. He was one of those
hail-fellow-well-met kind, a hand shaker and a back-
slapper. I don't like back-slappers and I didn't like him.
Generally the guy who slaps you on the back has a knife
in his paw. Nevertheless, I was pleasant to him and
laughed at all his stale gags. When you're on a business
deal that's what you've got to do. He looked the car over
carefully, had his mechanic drive it around the block,

and then made us an offer of $650.

Six hundred and fifty bucks—what a comedian! I laughed in his face. "Rock-bottom is eight hundred," I told him.

"Eight-fifty," interrupted Vera, shooting me a wicked look. "Eight-fifty or no sale."

That was the dealer's turn to laugh. He said that on second thought he couldn't give more than $625. Business was lousy, taxes unbelievable, overhead enormous. He went into a long song and dance about it. When he got done I told him in plain language where he could stick the $650, much less the $625.

"Is that a nice way to talk?" protested the dealer. "I've been doing business here for many years and my prices are fair. Why, I could name you..."

"Never mind naming anything. I'm not going to take an oriental jazzing from you or anyone else."

"And don't start telling us how you started in somebody's backyard," chipped in Vera.

"We're not interested. You second-hand car dealers are all alike. You sit in your shacks with your fingers crossed, waiting for a sucker to come along." She paused and ran a hand over a fender, admiring the paint-job. "You can have the car for $825. Take it or leave it."

I gave her the high-sign to keep out of it. "$775 and its yours. But not a cent less."

Than came the haggling. The dealer came up to $700, Vera came down to $790 and I began plugging seven and a half. We deadlocked there.

"Before I let it go for seven hundred, I'll wreck it and collect the insurance," stormed my sweet little wife.

The man got sore at that, and I can't say I blame him. "All right, forget it. I don't do business that way."

"Suit's me! Come on. Let's get out of this clip-joint." I let her lead me away a little. She was very upset and began to cough. I had to take her into the office for a drink of water. When she came out of the spell, she was white as a sheet. "Look, Vera," I said. "Take it easy.

You're going to gum the works. Let me handle this thing alone and I'll chisel every dollar possible. Sit down here and read the newspaper. If we go away now we'll only have to try some other guy."

Vera was very angry but she realized I was right. She told me in no uncertain terms what the dealer could take for himself and snatched up the newspaper. I stayed with her for a minute before going back.

"Your wife has quite a temper," observed the dealer.

"Yeah well to get down to business, you know damned well that car books for plenty. I'm no greenhorn. I want at least $750."

"Seven is tops, Mr. Haskell. My mechanic says she's pumping oil. Needs rings too, a valve job, a new head gasket and a general tune-up. That costs dough."

"But you've got a honey of a radio in there. Don't forget that."

"I'll give you $700."

"$740."

"$700."

We argued about thirty minutes longer, me building up, he tearing down. We went over every detail of the bus from stem to stern. I made him get down on his hands and knees to inspect the new rubber; I slapped him in the face with the special spot and foglights; I switched on the radio; I made him feel the swell leather upholstery; and before I got done I had the guy believing the buggy was a Rolls. When we were both completely worn out, we hit a compromise—his price, $700. We shook hands and he was just pulling out his blanks for the Motor Vehicle Department when Vera came out of the office.

"No sale," she said. "I've changed my mind."

"What!"

"I've decide we'd better keep the car, "she smiled. Come along, Charlie. I'll explain it to you later."

Disgust showed all over the dealer's face. "Well, I'll be..." he began.

The smile faded from Vera's eyes and they hardened

into that flinty glaze I had learn to fear. "Shut your mouth," she snapped at him. "I guess I can keep my own car if I want to."

"But Vera," I protested, "what the...?"

"You shut up, too. Come on."

I went along with her, not daring to cross her. That would have been a sucker play. God knows what she might let slip if we battled it out in public.

Driving home she sat quietly, refusing to answer my questions. However, when we arrived at the apartment, she showed me the newspaper she had been reading while I fought it out for second place with the dealer. A certain article provided interesting reading, especially since it was about me.

MAN'S BODY FOUND IN DITCH NEAR LOCKHART BY TELEPHONE LINESMEN

Police Suspect Foul Play

August 17th (AP) Yuma. Police here reported today the discovery of the body of a young man in a ravine bordering U.S. 70, approximately seven miles west of Lockhart Arizona. Telephone linesmen Paul Oak and G. Travell, who were repairing in the vicinity, were attracted to the remains by the abundance of buzzards continually alighting in the one spot. Descending the pole upon which they were perched, they made their way to the bottom of the ditch and stumbled over the remains, half covered with brush.

Calling the nearest State Police barracks, the linesmen then stood guard over the body until the authorities arrived from town. The body was that of a man of thirty to thirty-five, shabbily dressed. Marks on his forehead led the police to suspect he had been clubbed to death, or perhaps hurled from a speeding automobile.

Identification, the investigators admit, will be

difficult, due to the condition of the body. However, near the corpse searchers found a suit-case containing a soiled change of clothing and papers identifying the owner as one Alexander Roth. Police are busy checking this for possible clues.

No valuables were found. This is the fourth case of apparent homicide to be unsolved in the neighborhood, which is a desolate expanse of uninhabited wilderness and {Continued on page 32)

I tightened up as I continued to read. I wasn't accustomed to seeing my name in the paper. While the article was in the second section and squeezed in among a lot of cooking recipes, I had the feeling that now I was a public figure—too damned public to suit me.

I wondered if any of my old friends back in New York were reading about me and maybe saying what a shame it was I died so young.

And Sue... Holy Smokes! If Sue ran across that piece she would think I'd been murdered, too! I had to see her soon and let her know it was all a mistake. It would be cruel not to.

"Well," I said, looking up at Vera after I finishing the article for the third time. "I still don't savvy why you changed you mind about selling car. Seven hundred bucks is seven hundred bucks."

"Yes, I know," she replied, lighting a cigarette and smiling one of her poisonous smiles. "But seven million bucks, that's something else."

"Seven million!"

"Right the first time. Six naughts."

Was I right about her being wacky? Seven million dollars.

"Lady," I said, "maybe you've got the wrong idea. You own a Buick, not the factory. "

"Just turn the page."

I stared at her blankly.

"Go on. Turn it."

I did as she asked and instantly I knew what was up. The next page was the Society News, and while the printing was no larger than in the rest of the paper, the name Haskell leaped out and hit me between the eyes.

HASKELL NEAR DEATH

MILLIONAIRE EXPORTER IN CEDARS OF LEBANON, VICTIM OF PNEUMONIA

August 9th. Charles J. Haskell, noted sports enthusiast and president of the Wilmington and San Pedro Exports, Inc., lies close to death after a three weeks siege of bronchial pneumonia. Doctors have little hope of recovery...

I didn't have to read any more.

"I won't do it," I said.

"You will!"

"Damned if I will. Think I'm crazy?"

"You'll do it, all right."

"It's impossible, I tell you. No one could get away with an act like that. They'd be wise to me in a minute."

"Don't be yellow. You look enough like him. No kidding, you almost had me fooled for a while."

"Oh, Vera. Don't you think a father would know his own son? And there must be other relatives—the girl for instance. She'd find out."

"The father won't have to know you. We'll wait until he gives up the ghost. He's an old geezer. He won't pull through. And as far as the girl's concerned: she hasn't seen you in fifteen years or more. She couldn't have been older than eight or nine when you left. Now look, it's not as tough as it sounds. You've got all kinds of identification—the car, letters, his licenses..."

"I couldn't get away with it."

"The old boy has scads of dough. Look in the paper, here. Personal fortune assessed at over fifteen million! He'll leave plenty, I tell you."

"He may have cut off his son. How do we know? Nope, it's out, Vera. I won't have anything to do with it."

Seeing how determined I was, she began to play upon my sympathy. She told me all about herself and her past, little incidents that were touching, if they were true: how all her life she had been given the dirty end of the stick; how she had to slave for whatever she received, and how she had always been pushed around like an animal. Then, to top it off, an M.D. had pronounced her death sentence.

"Why do you think I was heading out west for?" she asked bitterly. "Because I want to break into movies and become Gertie Glamour? I'll tell you why, if you want to know. I'm out here for my health, that's why. The sawbones in Kansas City said I wouldn't last a year if I didn't get out to the right kind of climate. And even if I did, he said he couldn't promise much. Yes, that's right. My lungs. They're like Swiss cheese."

"Gee, that's too bad, Vera."

"Oh, I'm not crying about it. But you can bet your life I'm going to live before I croak. I'm going to have all those things they dangle before you in the movies, diamonds and fur coats and breakfasts in bed. I'm going to be just as stuck-up as the rest of them."

"But—"

"No, don't interrupt me, Roth. For the first time in my life I see a clear way to the big money; and you're going to help me, like it or not. I'm going to ride down Broadway in a Duesenberg, then across to East 100th Street. That's where I was born, Roth. Ever been over in that section? It's tough as hell there. A stranger takes a chance of getting his block knocked off if he walks through there at night. Well, there's a tenement on that street that I'm going to buy, see? I'm going to pay cash for it and put the landlord out on his heine, the way he put my mother out on hers. I'm going to..."

I let her rave on but her spiel didn't move me a bit. The more I considered her idea, the more ridiculous and impossible it looked. The chances seemed to grow longer, like Jack's beanstalk. Besides, there was Sue to think about. She was the soul of honesty, and even if I did get away with it, I'd be all washed up with her.

"I'm sorry, Vera. I'll do anything within reason. But not that. So forget it—or get yourself another stooge."

"You sap!" she yelled at me. "You'll be fixed for life as Charles Haskell. You can take your inheritance and go away. No more worrying about the rent. No more sweating and scheming and chiseling and wondering where your next meal's coming from. Think of that, Roth."

"I can earn my own living."

"Living? Do you call what you're doing living?"

I resented that remark. I wanted to tell her what a fine musician I was, how once I had brought down a high-school auditorium with a Brahms Concerto. I controlled myself, though. She'd never believe it. She'd only give me the horse-laugh.

"I get along," I said sullenly.

"I'll tell you what I'll do. I'll even split fifty-fifty with you." Darned big of her! She said that last as if she was making some big sacrifice. Sure. She was. The sacrifice was me. It wouldn't be any skin off her back if I was caught pulling the stunt. God bless her generosity—but nuts. "No. And that's final."

"We'll wait until we read that the old man's dead. Then you show up—as if you read in New York that he was sick."

"What if he doesn't die?" I didn't really care whether he died or not—because nothing she could say or do would make me go into a thing like that—but I was trying to punch holes in her brainstorm.

"He's sure to die. I know he will. Something tells me."
Something told me, too. Those Haskells were always
dying at the wrong time.

But as much as I insisted I was not going to have
any part of it, Vera was taking it for granted I would. She
didn't talk a great deal about it after her one outbreak,
but I could tell her mind was not on her cards when we
played casino that afternoon. She missed lots of moves
and I beat her easily. Not only that, I noticed that she
kept looking at Haskell's watch every few minutes. I was
aware that she was just trying to kill time between
newspaper editions.

As for myself, I was doing plenty of heavy thinking,
too. I knew Vera well enough by this time to realize she
was one of the most stubborn mules in the world. If she
thought an idea was good, she'd try it at any cost.

That meant I would have to prove to her it was
screwy... and it wouldn't be easy. That it was dangerous
and almost certain to end in disaster wouldn't bother her
much. All she had to lose was me.

"Vera," I pleaded, "don't you realize if I'm caught
they'll want to know where I got the car and stuff? Then
they'd have me on a murder rap."

"If you're smart, you won't get caught."

I hadn't counted much on that angle, so I tried
another.

"And if I am, don't you realize you'll be out, too?"

She seemed more interested in that. She looked up
from her hand immediately. "How will I be out?"

The bitch. I could get caught and hanged for all she
cared. But let her drop a dollar and it was a catastrophe.
"You'll be out the seven hundred we could have grossed
on the car."

She didn't say anything to that for a second and I
began to hope. A slight frown and narrowed eyes made it
clear that this bit of it had not occurred to her before.
"Really, Vera," I went on, "you'd be an awful chump to
throw away all that dough on a dizzy long-shot. Let me

sell the Buick tomorrow. With the money it'll bring, and with what you've already got, a clever kid like you can run it up in no time. Then we'd both be in the clear."

"I'd be in the clear anyway."

"Maybe, maybe. If I got caught I'd be good and sore at you, you know."

You mean you'd squeal?" I saw her eyes begin to blaze and I knew I'd put my foot into it. "No, not squeal, exactly. I meant.."

"Never mind what you meant. Even if you did tell the cops I was in it with you, what could they do to me? They might give me the same medicine they'd give you but I'm on the way anyhow. All they would be doing would be hastening it."

"All right. But think of the seven hundred you might lose. You'd kick yourself around the block if it got away from you."

She paused a moment before speaking. There was a little war going on inside her. Should she pocket her winnings or parley? "I'll take the chance," she said.

I shrugged, as if her decision made no difference to me. I didn't want to let her know that behind my mask I was furious. I felt like clipping her one and when she was on the floor taking that skinny neck in my hands and throttling her. "You're being foolish," I remarked, keeping my voice even. "That's how people wind up behind the eight-ball. Once they get a few dollars they become greedy and want more."

No reply to this.

"Caesar—you know, that Roman general—got his for being greedy. He wasn't satisfied and the final wind-up was he took the count."

Still no answer. I might as well have been talking to a stone wall. But it was a good sign, I thought. Maybe what I was telling her was sinking in (I hoped).

"A couple of days ago you didn't have a dime. Why, you were so broke you couldn't have gotten into a pay-toilet. Now you've got over seven hundred bucks with seven hundred more in the offing. Take my advice and don't try for more."

Vera's answer to that was a disgusted groan. She threw down her cards. "I'm tired of this game. Let's play Fantan." Realizing now that she hadn't even been listening to me, I burned and got up. "Play solitaire," I growled.

"O.K., if that's the way you feel about it."

"That's the way I feel about it." I flopped on the couch, yanked one of the pillows away and threw it into a far corner. It came close to knocking a picture off the wall.

"Getting sore and throwing things won't help, Roth. For Heaven's sake, I'm really doing you a favor. I help you out of a jam by keeping my mouth shut, I show you how to make yourself some soft money, and what thanks do I get?"

"Thanks?"

"Sure. Would you rather I call the cops and tell them you killed a man and stole his money?"

"I didn't kill anybody!"

"You did."

"I didn't, God damn it, and you know it!"

"All right, then. Suppose I call the police? If you're innocent, what have you got to be scared of?"

"Call them, you bitch! Go ahead, call them! See if I care. At least they'll give me a square deal!"

"You want me to call them?"

"You heard me. But I'm warning you. If I'm pinched, I'll swear you were in on it! I'll say you helped me! If I burn for it, I'll get even with you!"

"You wouldn't dare."

"No? Then try it and see. Call them." All this was about half an hour before she died and the conversation, while not particularly cool, was at least pitched low. However, as the minutes passed, and more obstacles to the plan popped into my head, the air got blue. Each word coming from our lips snapped like a whip.

I reminded her that as Charles Haskell I didn't even know my mother's name, whether Dolores' birthday was in September or May, where I had attended school, the name of my best friend, whether I had an Aunt Emma or not, if I had ever owned a dog, my religious denomination, or even what the "J" in my name stood for. I also pointed out that the original Haskell bore a scar on his wrist.

"His people never saw that scar," retorted Vera. "He told me he ran away right after putting out the kid's eye."

"Yes," I agreed heatedly, "but his father knew he was cut. There would have to be something on the wrist to show."

"So what? The old man's dead—or will be, I hope, by tomorrow morning's paper. Anyway, you could cut yourself a little, couldn't you? Christ, for seven million I'd let you cut my leg off."

"No. Turn me in, if you want, but I won't get mixed up in it. Besides, Haskell was a hop head. Maybe he wasn't the man's son at all. Maybe he dreamed all this, for all we know."

"Well, dream it or not, you won't be dreaming when the law lay hands on you. They've got a cute gas-chamber waiting for you, Roth—and extradition to Arizona is a cinch..."

"Go on, go on. You haven't the guts to call them!"

But, folks, she did. And if it was a bluff, it was a good one; because I fell for it, and that is exactly how it happened. She went to the phone, began calling the police and I strangled her to death.

Accidentally, though. Much as I feared and hated her, the last thing I wanted was for her to die. I was in enough trouble, liable to be suspected of a murder, without actually committing one. But when I heard her ask Information for the number of the Hollywood police station, heard her repeat it and heard her dial it, I rushed across the room and tried to get the receiver from her hand. Somehow, as we struggled for the thing, her throat got in the way. I grabbed on to it and squeezed. It was soft, much softer than I'd dreamed; because when she let the phone fall and slumped against me, I noticed the marks of my fingers, blue and deep. I let go of her then and she dropped to the floor. God, it's easy to kill a person.

The world is full of skeptics. I know. I'm one myself. In the Haskell business, how many of you would have believed me if I had allowed myself to be arrested and brought to trial? And now, after killing Vera without really meaning to do it, how many of you would believe it wasn't premeditated? In a jury room, every last one of you would go down shouting that she had me over a barrel and my only out was force. Accidents are accidents, mistakes are mistakes, but coincidence is baloney, no matter how you spell it.

All this became immediately clear to me in the minutes or seconds or hours that I stood over Vera's body, staring at it. I was like a kid, admiring his first bicycle—only it wasn't a bicycle and I wasn't admiring it. I was amazed and dreadfully shocked at what I saw.

The room was still, so quiet that for a time I wondered if I had suddenly gone deaf. Then, gradually, as my senses returned, sounds began to fill my ears: the rumble of a bus on Sunset Boulevard, the whine of a vacuum cleaner, the sour notes of a trumpet being practiced somewhere in the building, the blasting voice of a radio politician. All this added to my astonishment. Here I had just snuffed out a human life as easily as falling off a log and the world was going on the same as always. The sun was still shining, the birds singing, the people eating, sleeping, working, making love, spanking their children, patting their dogs. It was undeniable proof that man is unimportant in the scheme of things, that one life more or less doesn't make a hell of a difference.

Yet to me, who had taken a life and whose own life hung in the balance, this was crazy. God Almighty, I thought, man is important. A few seconds ago Vera was alive. Blood ran through her veins; saliva was in her mouth; she could feel things: the tickling sensation that made her cough now and then, the pimple on the lobe of her left ear.

Now she lay still and dead. That must mean something. It must! Why, if I died... But I couldn't imagine myself dying. I couldn't imagine not being me any more.

These thoughts ran through my mind rapidly and I could barely keep myself from running to the window and shouting, "Pipe down! Shut up! Don't you realize someone died? How would you like to die, you heartless sons of bitches?"

I was hysterical—but without making a sound. My eyes clung to Vera as she lay twisted on the floor, her legs sprawled out awkwardly. Her face was flushed. Her hands, crossed on her breast with the fingers at her throat, were stiff as boards. The fingers themselves were bloodstained—which made me conscious for the first time that my wrists were aching. Looking at them, I saw that they were scratched to ribbons. Believe me, if I could have laughed, I would have. Now I was Charles Haskell to a 'T. As Vera kicked off she had added the final touch. It was only three minutes by Haskell's watch, strapped to the dead woman's wrist, that I stood there looking down at her. It seemed hours. Her hair had fallen across her face, so, thank God, I couldn't see her eyes; but her mouth was a little open, as if she had been struggling to yell "Copper!" when death came. The little whore. I wasn't sorry she was dead; just sorry it was me who killed her. After a time, my eyes reluctantly left Vera and traveled around the room. It was in disorder for we hadn't straightened up after our drinking-bout the night before. Cigarette stubs were strewn on the carpet, some of them with lipstick on them. There was a broken glass by the couch. My pyjamas lay in a corner where I'd tossed them. The telephone was still on the floor with the receiver off the hook. Something warned me that it might be a good idea to replace it. Nevertheless, I couldn't budge.

I was aware that now, since I was undoubtedly a murderer, I had better be a successful one and not get caught. What evidence there was about the place had to be destroyed—and from the looks of things there was plenty. In a book, the murderer generally tries to pin the crime on someone else, the rat. Well, I didn't have anyone I could pin it on, so that was out. What first? Fingerprints. Surely everything was lousy with them. But where to begin? Where?

I started to wipe a table before I saw the phone, and then I began wondering if fingerprints can be detected in human flesh. I was nervous. My heart was sinking so fast it hurt. I thought that if only I could compose myself and treat it like a game, maybe I'd get away with it. I'd get a sheet or a blanket first and cover Vera up....

But as soon as I made a move towards the bedroom, the full realization dawned on me. There was no way out of this. I could polish off prints for ten years but there'd always be witnesses. The landlady, for one. She could identify me. Although we rented the place early in the evening and the transaction took place in a dim room without a light and Vera had done most of the talking, she most certainly noticed me. Then too, there was the car dealer. He could identify me. After Vera's demonstration of temper he wouldn't be likely to forget us for a long while. And the police. They might have received the call Vera put through. Even now they might be tracing it.

I listened for the sound of sirens.... Yes! That was one now! And it seemed to be coming.... No, no. That wasn't a police siren. Only that damned vacuum cleaner.

My nerves were shot to pieces. While once I had remained beside a dead body, planning carefully how to avoid being accused of murdering him, this time I couldn't. This time I was guilty—knew I was guilty and felt it. Stupid or not, I couldn't help doing the thing which once before I had managed not to do.

I ran.

VI. SUE HARVEY

When a person you have been very fond of passes away, you are supposed to cry—so I cried. However, hypocritical as it may seem, I didn't feel much like crying. I guess I was never really in love with Alex, for when I read he had been found dead in a ditch I was more relieved than anything else. It made things much less complicated. The article in the paper immediately blew away whatever fog had been obscuring my true feelings. I was very, very sorry about Alex—but it was Raoul I loved.

It is strange how something pretty terrible must happen before we can accurately analyze things and place them in their proper grooves. If Alex had remained alive, I might have gone on for years thinking I loved him. I might even have married him. Things we have grown accustomed to in this life we cling to long after they have ceased to function. It took the news of Alex's death to make me conscious he was only a friend.

Of course there is always a certain amount of sadness connected with a death—especially such a horrible one as had overtaken Alex. Nevertheless, it surprised and even annoyed me a little to find that Ewy, who had never even met the man, was taking it a good deal harder than I was. We were seated on the living-room divan with our arms around each other, and she was weeping on my neck rather than me weeping on hers.

In a picture, when the heroine's brother or boy friend dies—in an airplane or performing some act of bravery in the war—the accepted reaction no longer calls for a copious flow of tears, bosom beating and hair-tearing. That went over big in the silent days. Now there is little more than a perceptible stiffening of the shoulders, a dullness about the eyes, and some graceful, expressive gesture. In close-up, the mouth may twitch a trifle—but no more than just that. Whether this is how a person would react in real life or not, I don't know, never having experienced a truly overwhelming sorrow. The news that Alex was dead came as a shock—but after the shock passed there was nothing.

I am not trying to excuse myself for this cold blooded attitude by reminding you that in the four or five months I had been separated from him he had gone out of my life entirely. Nevertheless, such was the case. Hollywood is a peculiar spot. Once you're here, everything and everyone outside seems to be at the other end of the world. Live in Hollywood for a short while and then try to go home. You'll never be contented again. A week here will find you infected with that curious unrest that is so much a part of everyone in the colony. I could understand now why I seldom wrote letters to him. I had imagined that this was because I had nothing of interest to report, little dreaming that we were in the act of drifting apart and approaching permanent estrangement. His own letters to me, while always welcome, I now realized meant no more than a temporary escape from my problems.

So Alex was dead, poor lamb. And murdered. Well, this was not surprising. A violent death was quite in keeping since all his life Alex had been a pugnacious sort, picking fights with people upon the slightest provocation. I remembered the time he had been fired from his job for just such antics. Imagine hitting a customer—and on the dance-floor, of all places. Oh, he thought he was doing me a favor, of course, upholding my honor and all that sort of rubbish. In reality, if he'd only known it, it caused nothing but trouble. Bellman warned me that if I had any more admirers with tempers like that he'd have to dispense with my services. Why do men persist in the belief that women relish brutality? That type of thing went out with the Stone Age.

And that he should have died in Arizona also was

not very surprising. Without a doubt he had been on his way out to see me, as I had begged him to do many times. From the looks of things, he had met up with bad company, become involved in a brawl on the road and someone had blackjacked him.

My motto has and always will be: What is done is done. Therefore, after several minutes allotted to getting over the shock, I dabbed at my eyes and ceased thinking of him. He had been very sweet and considerate; but people die every day and, no matter how much they may have meant, life, like the show, must go on.

Now I would have to concentrate on Raoul, whom I loved. If he in turn loved me—as I was positive he did—he must marry me before leaving for New York. Hollywood was more sickening than ever. The studios were still impregnable fortresses, so near and yet so far beyond reach. Then, too, I suddenly remembered I no longer had a job. Damn Selma.

Well, I mused, maybe it was for the best. Back East I could land something in a minute, and with Raoul appearing in the new Harris production we'd be doing fine. But no more ruining my arches for Bellman. I'd wait until something decent turned up—a show job, or even a spot in the Paradise Restaurant chorus. This decided, and with my mind made up to be gone from Hollywood in a week, I began contemplating married life as Mrs. Kildare. But would he be willing to marry me? That was a dubious point. For some reason people in the profession regard marriage as a snare which is set to trap and extract their various personalities. The very thought of sacred bonds west of Vermont Avenue is abhorrent.

Well, abhorrent or not, Raoul would marry me or I'd know the reason why. I'd think of angles. I patted Ewy on the head, pushed her away gently and rose from the divan.

"Get me up in the morning, honey," I said softly. "Before you leave for the studio be sure I'm out of bed. And now we'd better turn in. It's after three."

As I led her into the bedroom, still weeping, she turned towards me. "God, you're taking it bravely," she choked.

There are various ruses a girl may employ in wooing a man to the point of proposal. These are not new innovations, despite the hypocrisy of our grandmothers. Women have chosen and pursued their men since the beginning of time although they have graciously permitted the victim the misconception that they merely submitted.

On my way to the hospital the next afternoon I considered these methods, discarding the most effective at once because it is nasty. Not only that, it defeats its own purpose. Sooner or later the man is bound to discover he has been duped and will see to it that life is made miserable for the girl—unless, of course, she really has a baby.

The second of these is purely psychological: play up to the fellow's ego (they all have them); make him conscious how weak and helpless you are to battle life alone; paint a grim picture of your present surroundings, taking pains of course, to hide your new fur coat; and make the future look exceedingly black—at the same time insisting that you thoroughly dislike the idea of marriage. But, by all means, never let him suspect you are leading him on.

And, lastly, is complete frankness—disarming if inadvisable, however a great time-saver. I decided that since the time element was so important to me—not having a job or even the remotest prospect of one—I'd come right out and tell him bluntly I wanted him to marry me. If he loved me he wouldn't find this objectionable. If he didn't—well, plenty of time to think of that later.

Still, in all I was a little timid about proposing cold. I

was brought up in the crinoline tradition. Ladies, to my mother's way of thinking, should be little more than animated dishcloths, tea-pourer's and bridge-fiends. Even on Leap Year she would have committed hara-kiri before asking an old friend to dance with her. Her instructions were that I take what I want only when it was formally offered to me, replete with red tape and Emily Post. Consequently, you can understand, it was a mighty nervous girl who stood beside Raoul's wheel-chair on the hospital sunroof.

"Why, what is it, darling?" he asked. "You're jumpy as a cat. Is something troubling you?"

Knowing now that I loved him, he had regained much of his poise, his sense of humor and his phony English accent. However, now he had a sincerity about him and the overbearing manner to which I objected before was missing.

"No-o-o," I replied.

What was the sense, trying to kid myself. I couldn't do it. Each time I came to the point I stopped. It wasn't that I was bashful, exactly; it was just that I knew I couldn't make it sound right. Putting a hand on his arm, looking him squarely in the eye and saying: "Will you marry me?" was a speech for a man or for a Lesbian.

"That's good, sweetheart. Everything's going to be all right from now on. Once we get to New York...."

A good sign. Knock wood. I was going to New York with him.

"... and I land that part in the Harris show, we'll be sitting on top of the world."

"Won't we though?" I sighed, loud enough for him to hear me. "It'll be swell, being together."

"Scrumptious. "

"We've got to make plans."

"Yes. Oh, I've made some already. I'll have to get two new tires for the Caddy before we leave. Retreads. And say, I'm short a suitcase. Have you room in your luggage for my tennis and riding kit?"

"Of course. I'm going to throw out a lot of my junk. I need new clothes and plenty of them. Oh, Raoul, isn't it wonderful! Just think how seldom two people who love each other come together. It's so lucky our paths crossed. Why, if I hadn't taken that temporary job at Bloomberg's—as I almost didn't—and you hadn't driven in..."

"I would never have met you."

"Wouldn't it have been awful?"

"I can't conceive of it."

"We should be so grateful, darling. And I know everything's going to turn out fine for us. Just think—only the two of us."

He bit his lip absently. "Yes, the two of us..."

"You and I..." I murmured, lowering my eyes a la Merle Oberon and squeezing his hand. Hope, at the moment, was strong. I took note of his furrowed brows indicating deep thought, and of his mouth which he opened and shut several times as if he was starting to say something.

"Sue," he said at last, after a few minutes of silence, "I'd like to ask you—"

"Yes?" Breathlessly, breathlessly, breathlessly. Surely now he was about to pop that welcome question. Or wasn't he?

"I'd like to ask you if you think it's wise paying my back Guild dues, seeing that I'm leaving for New York?"

I dropped his hand and turned to face him squarely. That was all I needed. "Raoul. Are you or are you not going to marry me?" I demanded.

He gaped at me speechlessly for a minute, his face registering perfectly all the emotions necessary to an actor: surprise, horror, pathos, humor. He didn't seem to know what to say, whether to laugh, cry, or both.

"Do... do you mean it?" he managed to get out.

"Of course I mean it!"

"Yes, yes. I... I rather thought you did. Well..." He paused, fumbling for words. His face was pale and drawn. But I was in no mood for evasion. He was on the spot and I intended to keep him there until I got a definite answer. "Well what? Are you or not?"

"Why... why, yes. Yes, of course, Sue. Only..."

I kissed him on the mouth. "Oh, Raoul you've made me so happy. I never knew I could love anyone like this."

"I love you, too. Only Sue..."

"We can go down-town as soon as you're discharged from here and get the license. It takes three days, you know."

"Yes. I know."

I kissed him again and this time I really enjoyed it. However, I noticed that he was pulling away from me slightly.

"Now wait a minute, Sue. There's something you don't understand. We can't get married immediately."

"Of course we can't, silly. In California you have to wait....

"Anywhere we'd have to wait. You're forgetting, aren't you?"

"Forgetting what?"

"Selma. We were never divorced."

The world came up and hit me on the chin. Selma. Selma, of all people. She was his wife.

"We're only separated, you know."

"Oh."

"Now you understand, don't you?"

"Yes. Yes, of course. I understand perfectly."

"But I'll speak to her before we leave. She's not a bad sort. As long as I pay for it, she'll file suit. "

"Yes."

"I knew you'd understand."

And pulling me down to my knees beside his chair, he stroked my forehead and made pretty speeches, all about how beautiful I was, and how sweet, and how I affected him. The dialogue might have been by Shakespeare, for all I cared. I wasn't even listening.

No one will ever live to see the day that Sue Harvey

takes anyone else's left-overs—especially Selma's. I don't like second-fiddle, even in a symphony orchestra. Therefore, before I came out of the hospital, my mind was made up to forget Raoul Kildare. Whatever I had lost in pursuing my career, at least I still had my pride.

But I was hurt, for I loved him. Isn't it always the case? Things you don't care about are offered to you by the dozen; something you really want is denied you. This is a very nasty world we live in.

I walked all the way home, completely ignoring the fact that I still was required to finish up the week at Bloomberg's. I think better while walking, you see, and I was racking my brain to find some way to even up the score with that low, good-for-nothing Selma. But it didn't take much thinking. Fortunately, by the time I reached Western Avenue, I had the inspiration. The beauty of it was it would only cost a penny to do hundreds of dollar's worth of damage.

I went into the drugstore at the corner of Western and Franklin and bought a post-card.

Dear Mr. Bloomberg (I wrote). I believe you have a strict rule about employing married women. You discharged Gwen Fisher the other evening for this reason, if you recall. Yet you still keep Selma Nicholson, who is the wife of an actor by the name of Kildare. Is that what you consider fair play?

Leaving it unsigned, I dropped it into a mailbox. That took care of that.

Feeling much better about everything now, I continued to walk home. Was it wrong to do such a thing? Should I, as in the Bible, have turned the other cheek? Only a fanatic like my mother would practice that. I'm no angel.... Besides, Selma was married, wasn't she? There are too many single, unsupported girls out of work as it is. Bloomberg was absolutely right in not hiring married help. It was my duty to... Oh, hell. Of course, duty had nothing to do with it. I just wanted to get back at her and this was the only way that presented itself.

Ewy must have arrived home from work and gone out again before I came in, because there were three notes for me: one on the bed, one in the middle of the living-room rug, and one in the bathroom. The first one requested that I be very quiet coming in that night; number two was to the effect that Mr. Fleishmeyer of the Fleishmeyer Agency had phoned and left a message that I call him whenever I came in; while number three stated that Ewy had won $57.40 on a horse called Paradisaical which had nosed out one called Easy Cash back in New York. It went on to say that she would pay me what she owed in the morning. There was a five-dollar bill pinned to the note which, Ewy said, I might need in the meanwhile. I put the money in my purse and decided to go down to the Boulevard. The bungalow was getting on my nerves. If I stayed in I would only begin brooding about Raoul. In any event, there were some slacks I wanted to buy at the Sport Shoppe.

But before I left the bungalow, I went to the telephone and dialed a number.

"Hello. Mr. Fleishmeyer, please. Miss Harvey calling." A wait. "Hello, Manny. How are you? What? Oh, nothing much, really. Just been in a rut. Something came up that's kept me busy for a week. Oh no. Nothing like that. Just some personal business. Unimportant. What's new with you? Yes... yes... yes... yes. No! Really! At Selznick? Do you think you can? Oh, Manny, that's wonderful! When? On Thursday? Sure, I will. Wait, I want to jot that down. Thursday morning—ten o'clock report to wardrobe—test on Stage 4—what? Oh, will you pick me up? Fine. That's sweet of you, Manny. Thanks. What's that? Tonight? Surely, I'd love to. It's been ages, hasn't it? But that's Hollywood for you. You lose track of everyone. Come about eight-thirty, dear. I'll promise to be ready by then. Oh, all right. Make it seven-thirty if you insist on buying my dinner. O.K. Until seven-thirty then, Manny. Good-bye."

I hung up with a sigh. A test at last. But the thought of it didn't thrill me the way it is supposed to thrill an aspirant. Probably that was because I knew that tonight....

I was just preparing to leave when Ewy came in breathlessly. "Oh, Sue! Did you read my note?"

"Which one?"

"Sue, I won $57.40 on a crazy tip Joe Krauss gave me, Paradisaical in the fourth at Belmont Park! Just think! $57.40!" She stopped suddenly, the excitement draining from her face. "Say, what are you doing home at this hour? You're late for work. It's almost five."

"I'm fired."

I hadn't thought to tell her before. As a matter of fact, I rarely told her anything. While Ewy was certainly my closest friend—if I had any friends at all—I don't believe in confiding in people. I hadn't even told her about Raoul.

"You're fired?"

"Yes. But I've got a test on Thursday over at Selznick's. It may mean a contract. That's what Fleishmeyer was calling about."

"Oh, I see."

I could tell by the sound of her voice that Ewy was disappointed. "Now don't start raving about it. What am I out here for? To carry hot-dogs? This is a big chance and I'm not going to let it slip by."

"I didn't say anything, did I?"

"No, but you were getting ready to. What the hell,

Ewy? Fleishmeyer likes me. He can get me in places I'd never get in myself."

"Yes. "

"I want to get somewhere."

"Yes. "

"What are you crying about?" I asked as a tear slipped down one of her cheeks. "Don't be a fool."

"I'm not crying, Sue. I'm happy you're going to get a break, that's all."

"That's the spirit."

"Only... "

"Only what?"

"Only I can't see..." And here she really broke down and sobbed openly. "... I can't see how you can do this so soon after poor Alex—"

"Oh, shut up about Alex," I cut in furiously. Why did Ewy have to be like that? "I don't want to hear that name mentioned again, understand?"

"All right, Sue."

"Can't you understand that I'm trying to forget him? You little imbecile!"

Then, quite by accident, I fell into the lines of Journey's End, Captain Stanhope speaking.

"Good God, don't you think there are limits to what a person can bear? I want to forget, you fool, forget!"

Ewy stopped her sobbing at once and raised her face to mine.

"I'm sorry, Sue. I didn't understand. I'm sorry. Please forgive me. I didn't..."

"All right. Only I want to be alone. I'm going out."

I turned abruptly, brushing my eyes, snatched up a coat and left the bungalow.

Not bad, I thought to myself. Not bad at all. I was an actress. And I am.

VII. ALEXANDER ROTH

There is nothing so much like one road as another road, and any road but U.S. 70 and one going either to Los Angeles or New York was right for me. I had to get going—where, it didn't matter—and keep going. I was in Bakersfield before I read that Charles J. Haskell, Sr., was dead; and in Frisco before Vera's body was discovered; and in Seattle before the fifteen bucks I borrowed on Haskell's ring gave out. I felt somewhat easier in Seattle, hard up or not; because it was in Seattle that I read the following article:

HUSBAND SOUGHT BY POLICE OF THREE STATES

Charles Haskell, Wanted By Investigators for Questioning in Regard To The Afton Place Murder Still Missing.

August 22nd. (UP) Charles Haskell, New York bookmaker and husband of the murdered woman, Vera Haskell, is still at large. For the past week police have been checking into the clues found in the apartment of the strangled woman and in the automobile parked in the apartment house garage.

Is that one for the book or is that one for the book? Haskell gets me into a spot and Haskell gets me out of it. They even went so far as to print his picture, wired from

New York! It is easy to figure out how it happened, but if you can explain why it did, you're a better man than I am, Gunga-Din.

Vera was murdered by a dead man. Laugh that off. Nevertheless, when you come right down to it, my problems weren't solved. I had to stay away from Los Angeles for fear someone might recognize me—and I couldn't go back to New York because Alexander Roth was dead. That meant Detroit, Peoria, New Orleans and Butte no more. And that meant the end of my career before it was begun. Now I'd never stand under the lights and roll them in the aisles with Wagner, Schubert and Bach.

Not so bad, considering what I was escaping? I don't know about that. For me to throw away my ambitions to be a great musician is not the same as you putting out the cat or throwing away the Christmas tree. It was killing my soul, if that's what you call it; to keep my body alive.

And another thing. I was giving up Sue, which hurt me still more. I could never come near her with a thing like this hanging over my head. It hurt, as I said; yet there was a certain satisfaction in what I was doing. I was aware that giving up the only girl I ever loved, and the only one who'd ever loved me, was maybe the first decent thing I'd ever done. If I sent word to her, and she came running to me to be my wife, it would be hell on her the rest of her days. Thank God I loved her enough to make this sacrifice.

So here I am—one day in Buffalo and the next in Columbus, earning a couple of dollars now and then by rubbing out the hot stuff in cheesy bands. I keep trying to forget what happened—and I have, almost—except that once in a while I wonder what might have taken place and what my life might have been if that damned grey roadster hadn't stopped. And when I start wondering—well, sometimes I want to curse and sometimes I want to cry.

Dramatics, buddy? No, sir. No dramatics. God or Fate or some mysterious force can put the finger on you or on me for no good reason at all.

CPSIA information can be obtained
at www.ICGtesting.com
Printed in the USA
BVHW070423230122
626864BV00005B/630